THE FISHERMAN AND THE GENIE

STONE ARCH BOOKS
a capstone imprint

THE FISHERMAN AND THE GENIE

RETOLD BY **ERIC FEIN**

ILLUSTRATED BY **EDUARDO GARCIA**

DESIGNER: **HILARY WACHOLZ**

EDITOR: **DONALD LEMKE**

ASSOC. EDITOR: **SEAN TULIEN**

ART DIRECTOR: **BOB LENTZ**

CREATIVE DIRECTOR: **HEATHER KINDSETH**

EDITORIAL DIRECTOR: **MICHAEL DAHL**

Published by Stone Arch Books, A Capstone Imprint 151 Good Counsel Drive, P.O. Box 669 Mankato, Minnesota 56002 www.capstonepub.com Copyright © 2011 by Stone Arch Books All rights reserved. No part of this publication may be reproduced in whole or in part, or stored in a retrieval system, or transmitted in any form or by any means, electronic, mechanical, photocopying, recording, or otherwise, without written permission of the publisher.

Cataloging-in-Publication Data is available on the Library of Congress website.

ISBN: 978-1-4342-2134-6 (library binding)
ISBN: 978-1-4342-2777-5 (paperback)

Summary: The legendary tale of an evil Persian king, who marries a new wife each day and then kills her the next morning. To stop this murderous ruler, a brave woman named Scheherazade risks her own life and marries the king herself . . . but not without a plan. On their wedding night, she will entertain him with the tale of the Fisherman and the Genie — a story so amazing, he'll never want it to end.

Printed in the United States of America in Stevens Point, Wisconsin.
032010
005741WZF10

CONTENTS

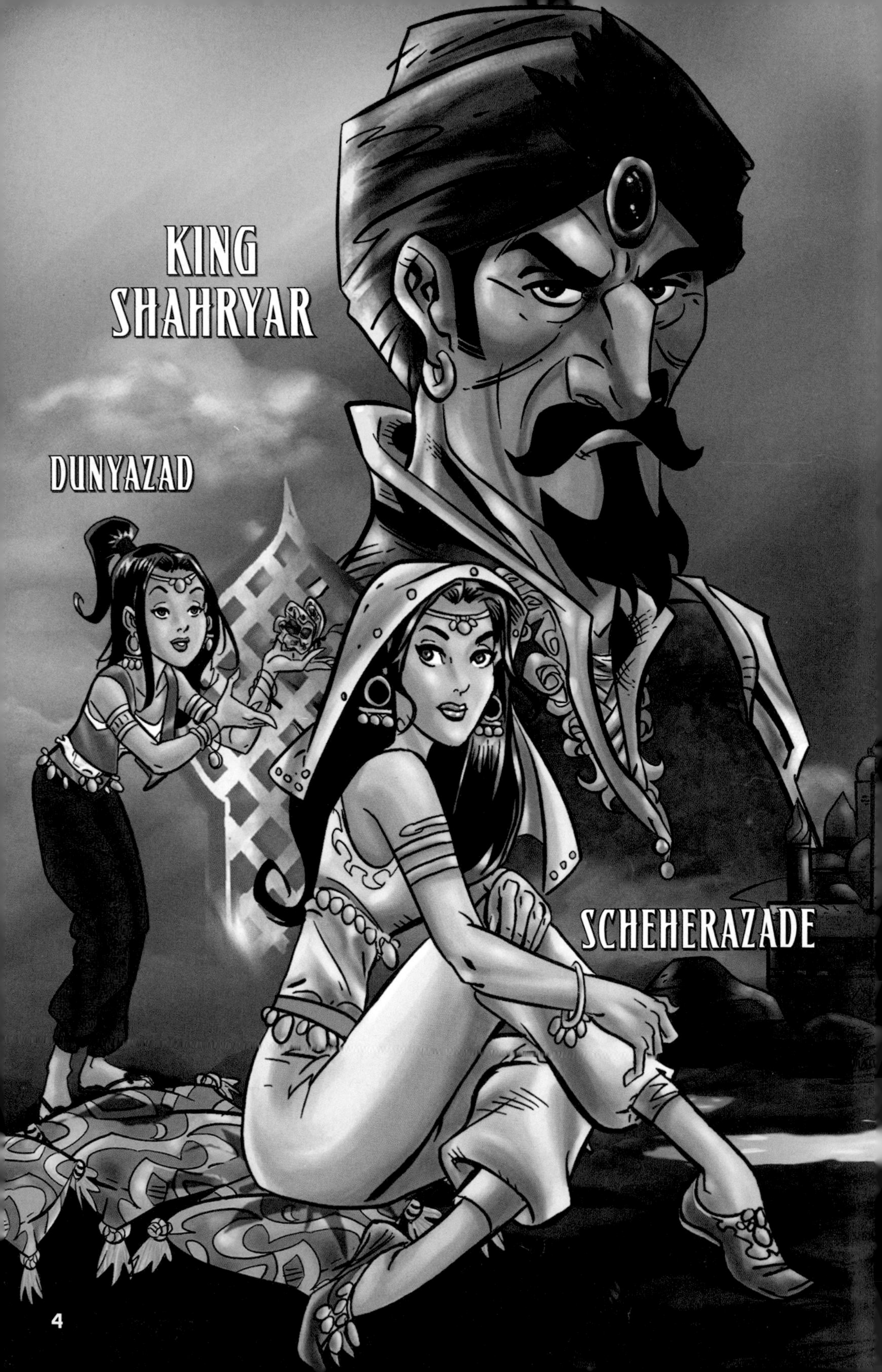
KING SHAHRYAR
DUNYAZAD
SCHEHERAZADE

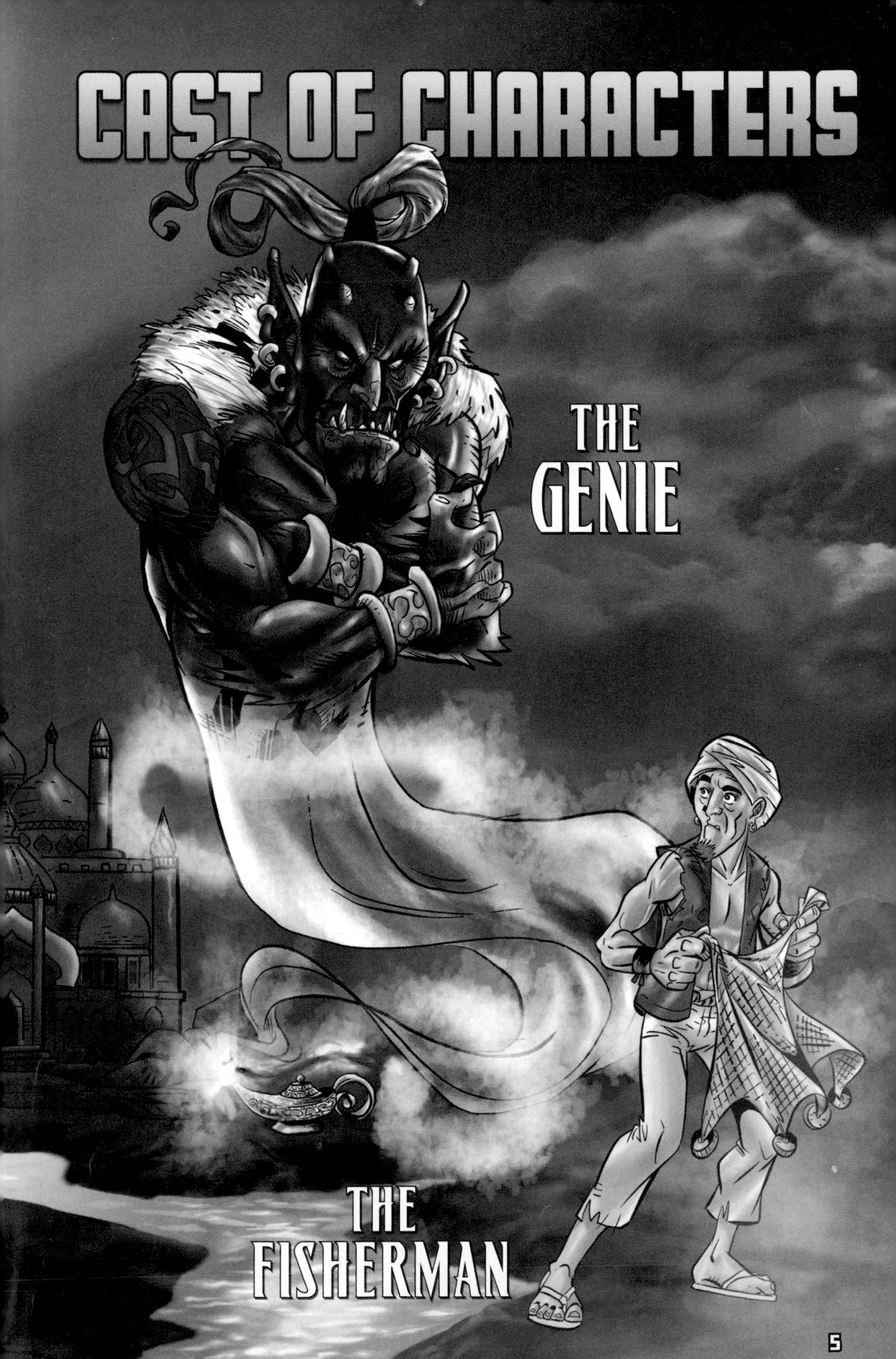
CAST OF CHARACTERS
THE GENIE
THE FISHERMAN

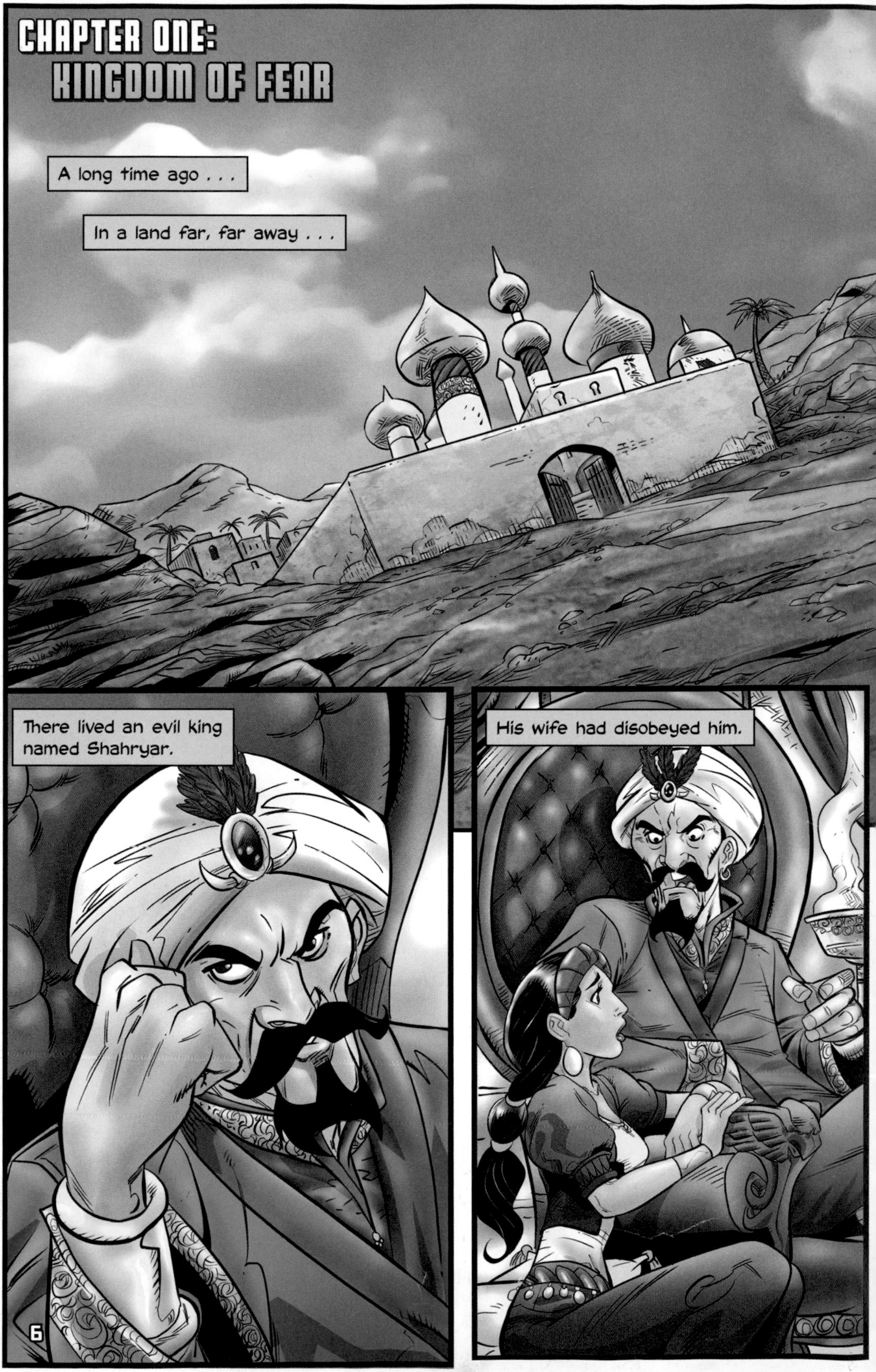
CHAPTER ONE:
KINGDOM OF FEAR
A long time ago . . .
In a land far, far away . . .
There lived an evil king named Shahryar.
His wife had disobeyed him.

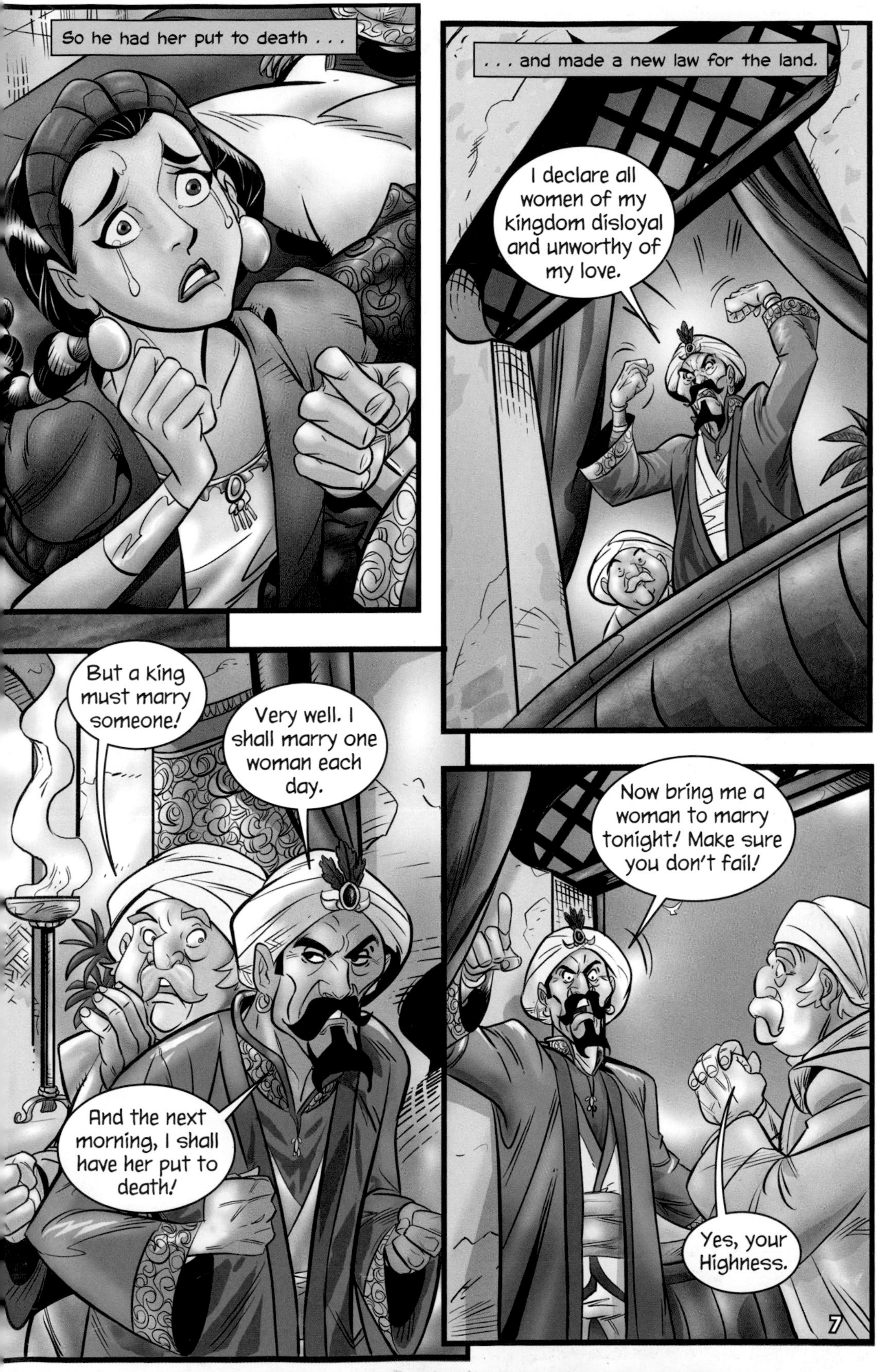

So he had her put to death . . .
. . . and made a new law for the land.
I declare all women of my kingdom disloyal and unworthy of my love.
But a king must marry someone!
Very well. I shall marry one woman each day.
And the next morning, I shall have her put to death!
Now bring me a woman to marry tonight! Make sure you don't fail!
Yes, your Highness.

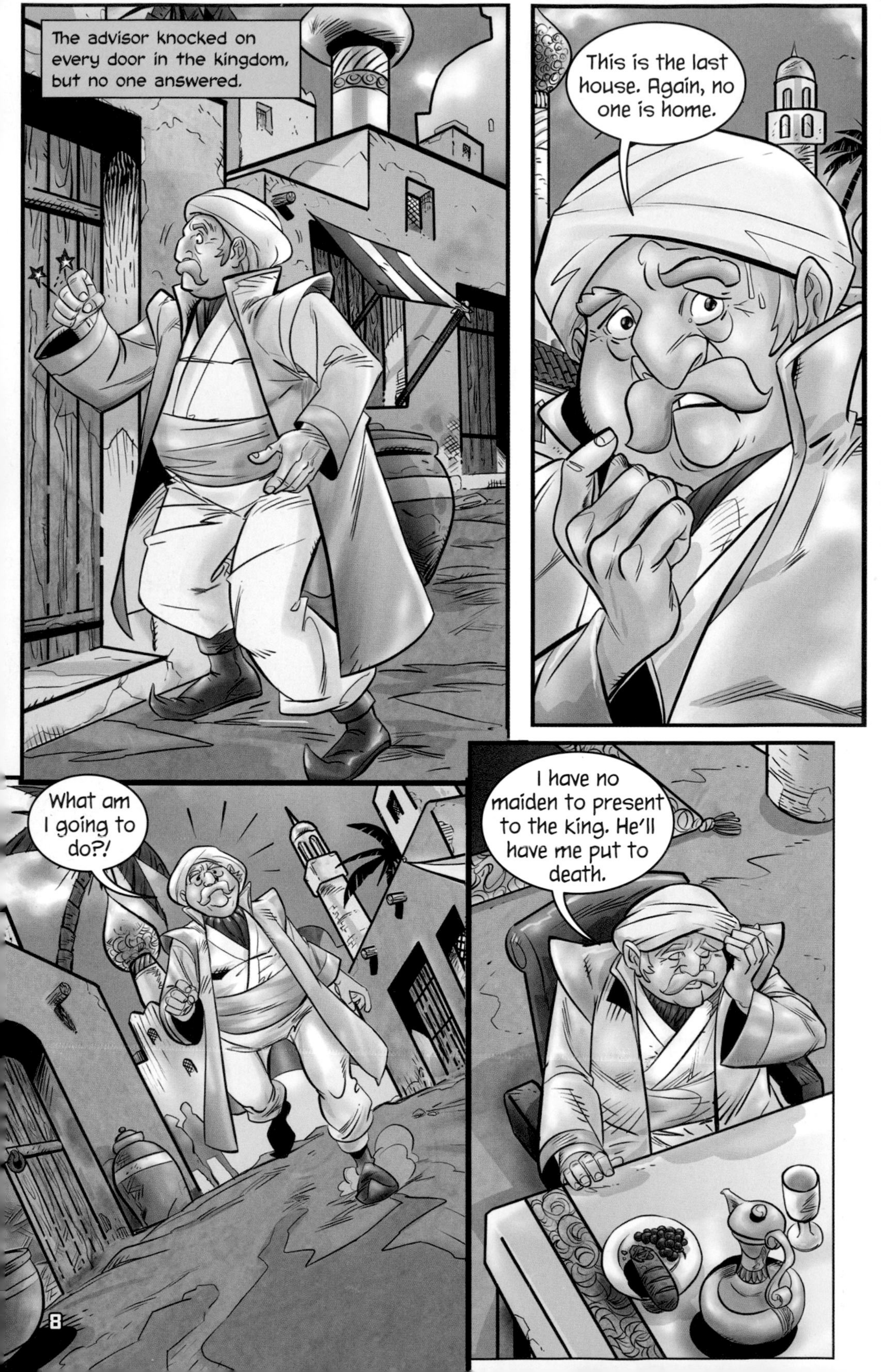
The advisor knocked on every door in the kingdom, but no one answered.
This is the last house. Again, no one is home.
What am I going to do?!
I have no maiden to present to the king. He'll have me put to death.

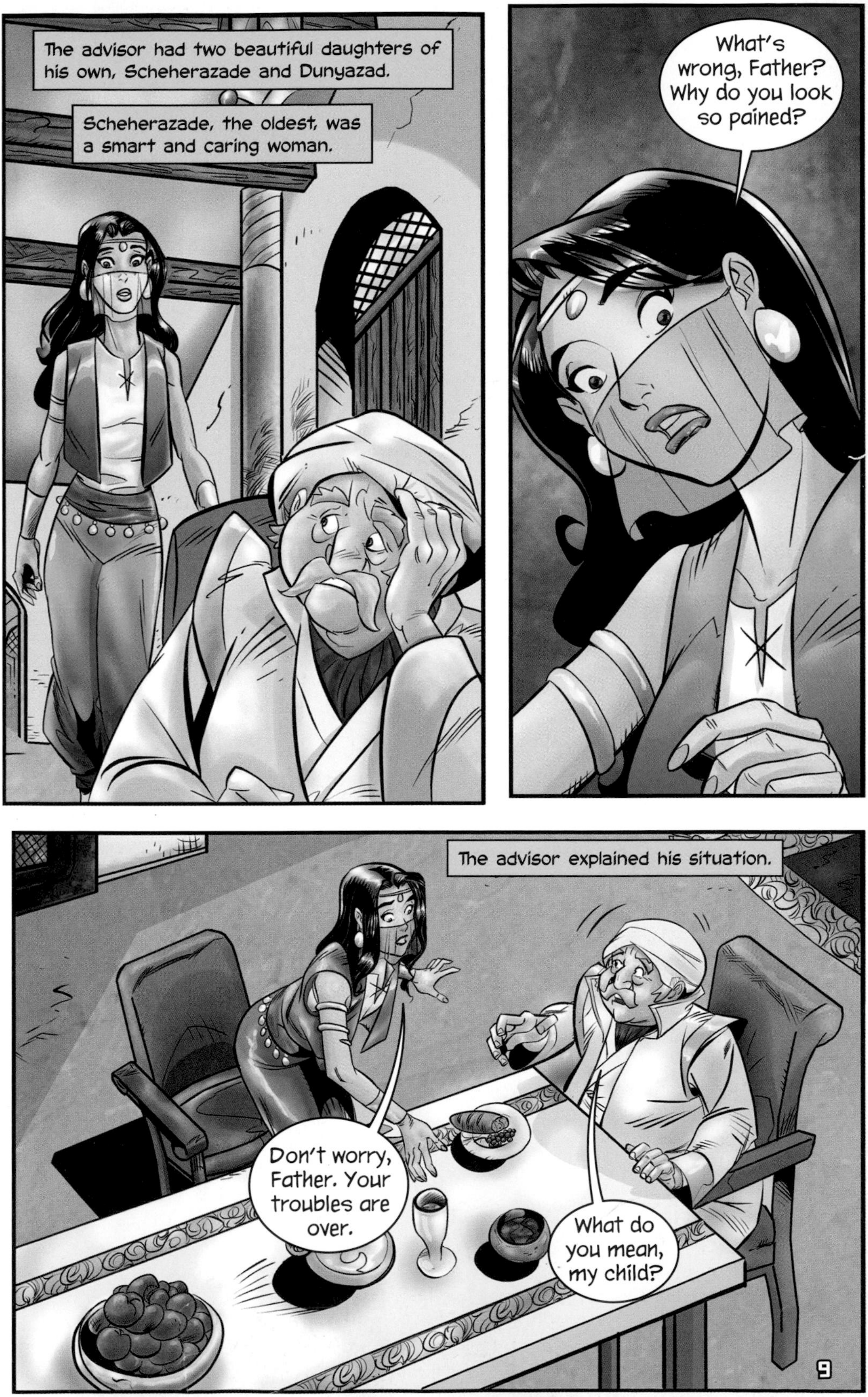
The advisor had two beautiful daughters of his own, Scheherazade and Dunyazad.
Scheherazade, the oldest, was a smart and caring woman.
What's wrong, Father? Why do you look so pained?
The advisor explained his situation.
Don't worry, Father. Your troubles are over.
What do you mean, my child?

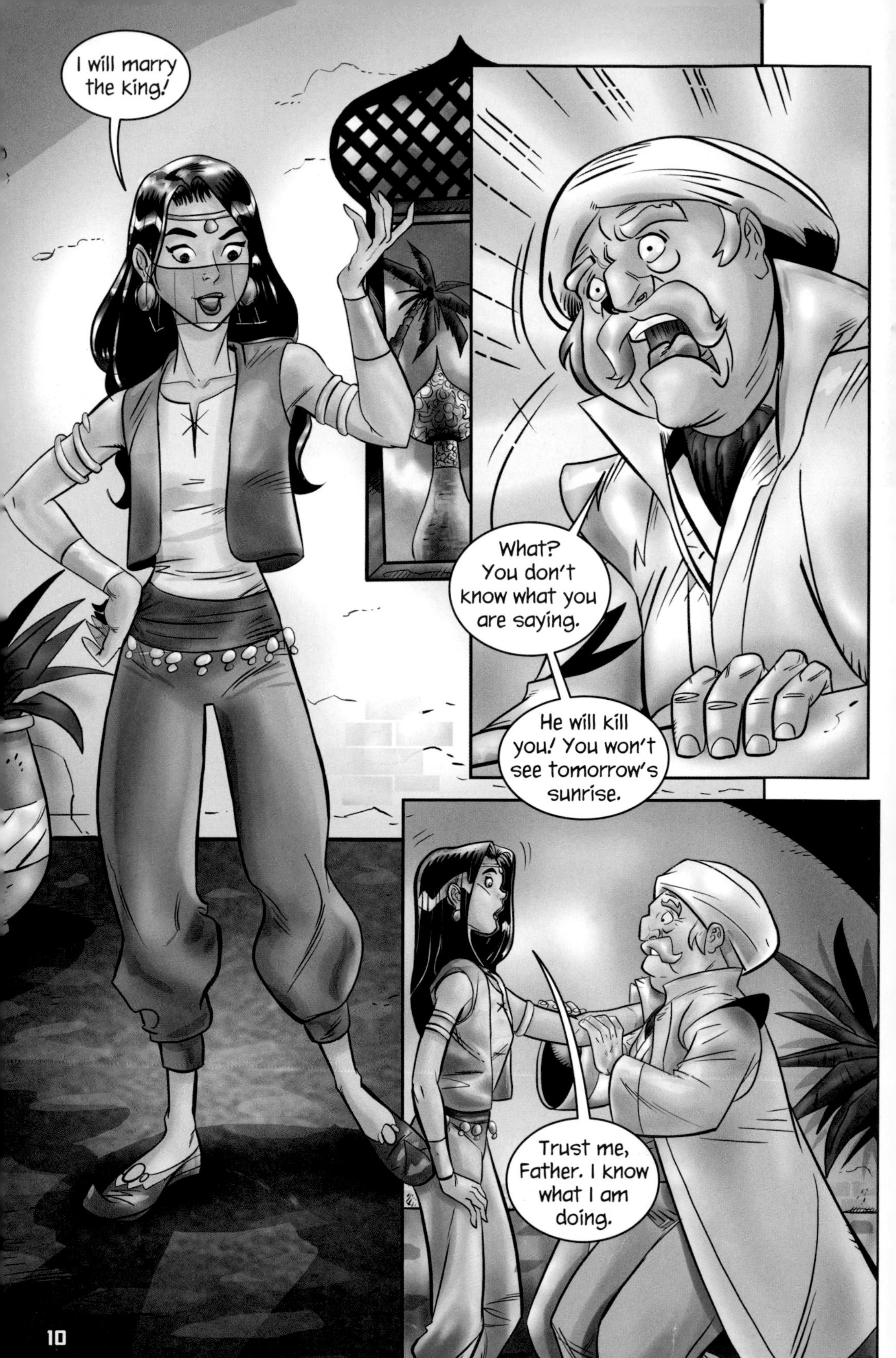
I will marry the king!
What? You don't know what you are saying.
He will kill you! You won't see tomorrow's sunrise.
Trust me, Father. I know what I am doing.

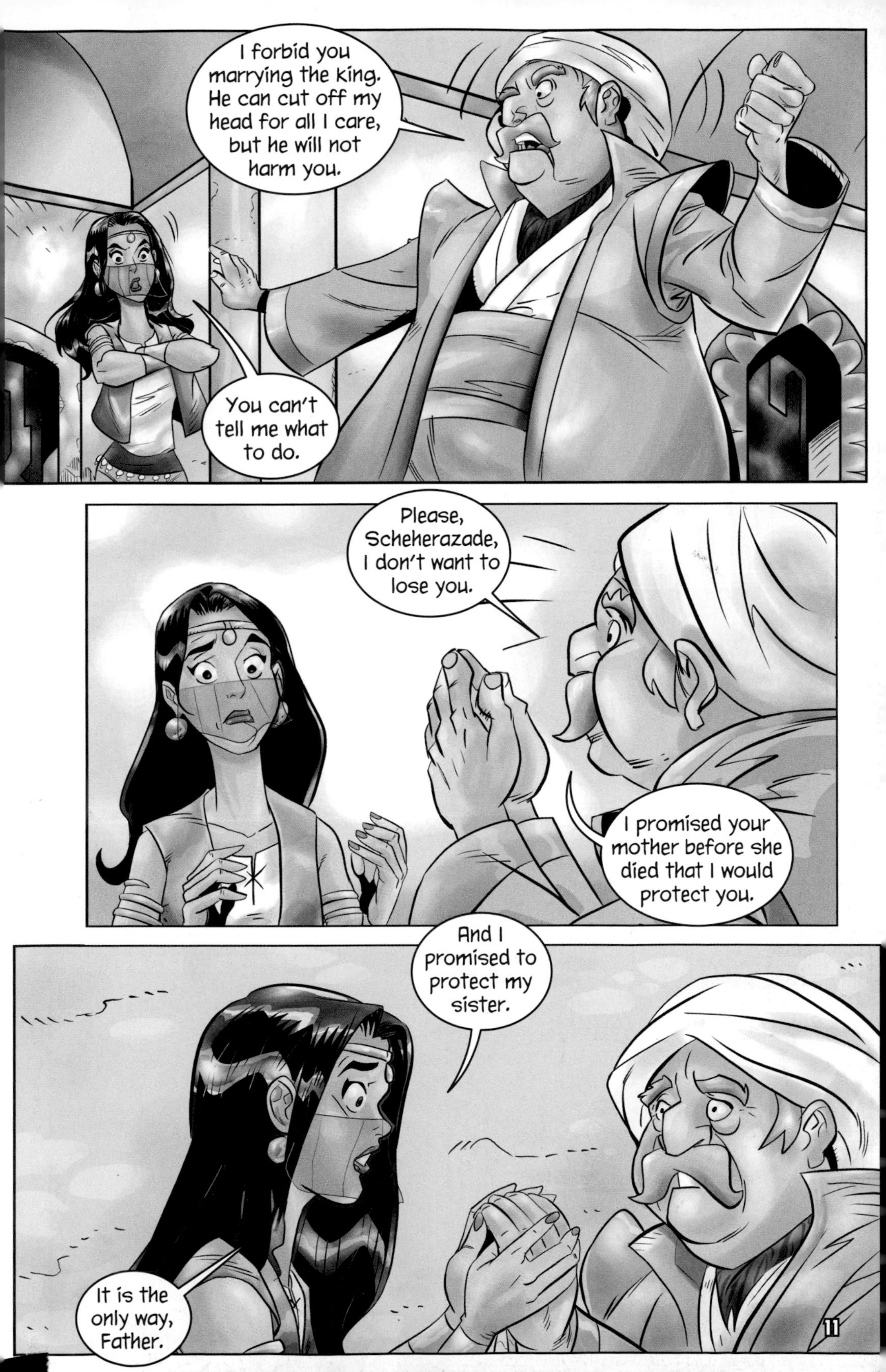
I forbid you marrying the king. He can cut off my head for all I care, but he will not harm you.
You can't tell me what to do.
Please, Scheherazade, I don't want to lose you.
I promised your mother before she died that I would protect you.
And I promised to protect my sister.
It is the only way, Father.

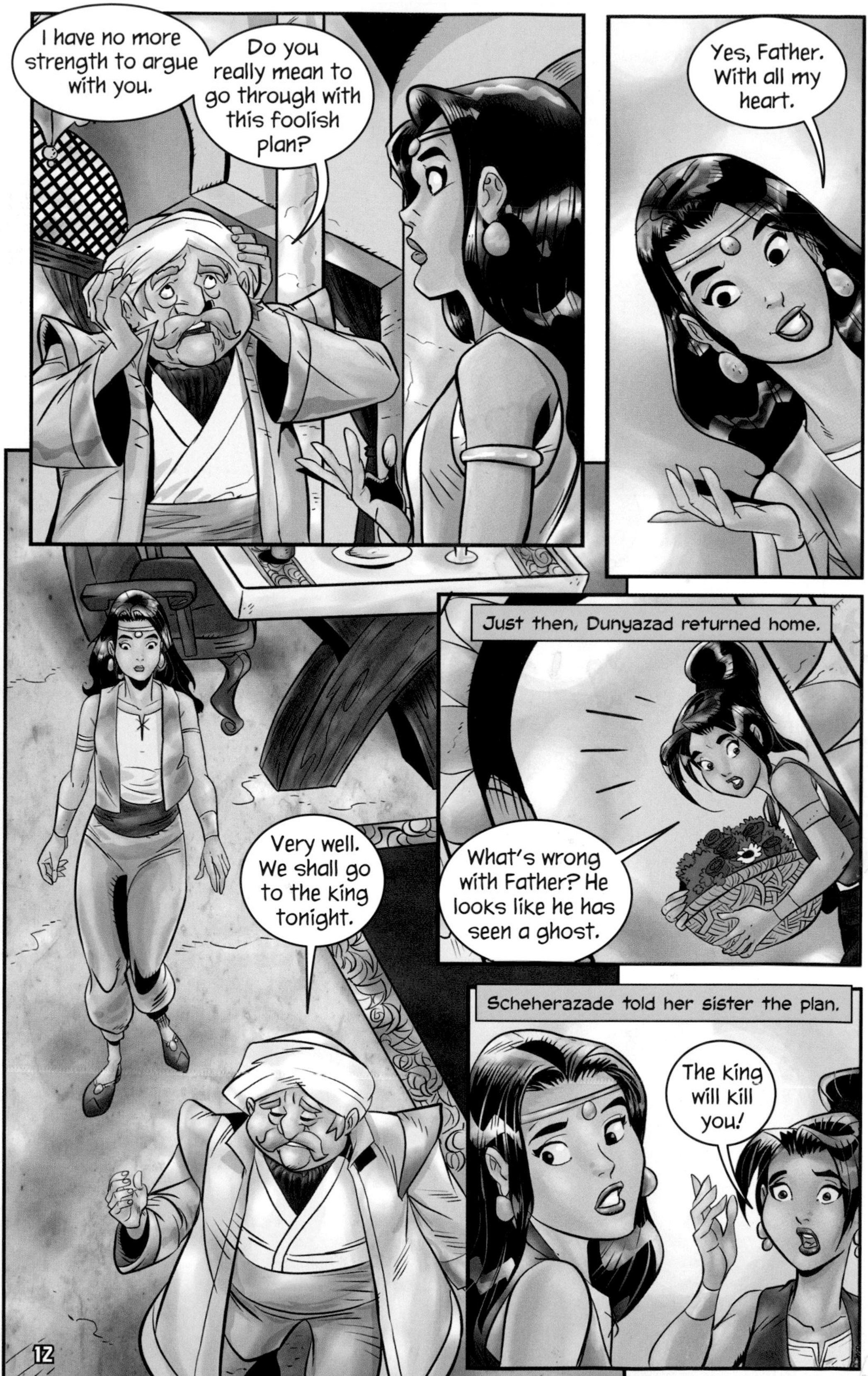
I have no more strength to argue with you.
Do you really mean to go through with this foolish plan?
Yes, Father. With all my heart.
Just then, Dunyazad returned home.
What's wrong with Father? He looks like he has seen a ghost.
Very well. We shall go to the king tonight.
Scheherazade told her sister the plan.
The king will kill you!

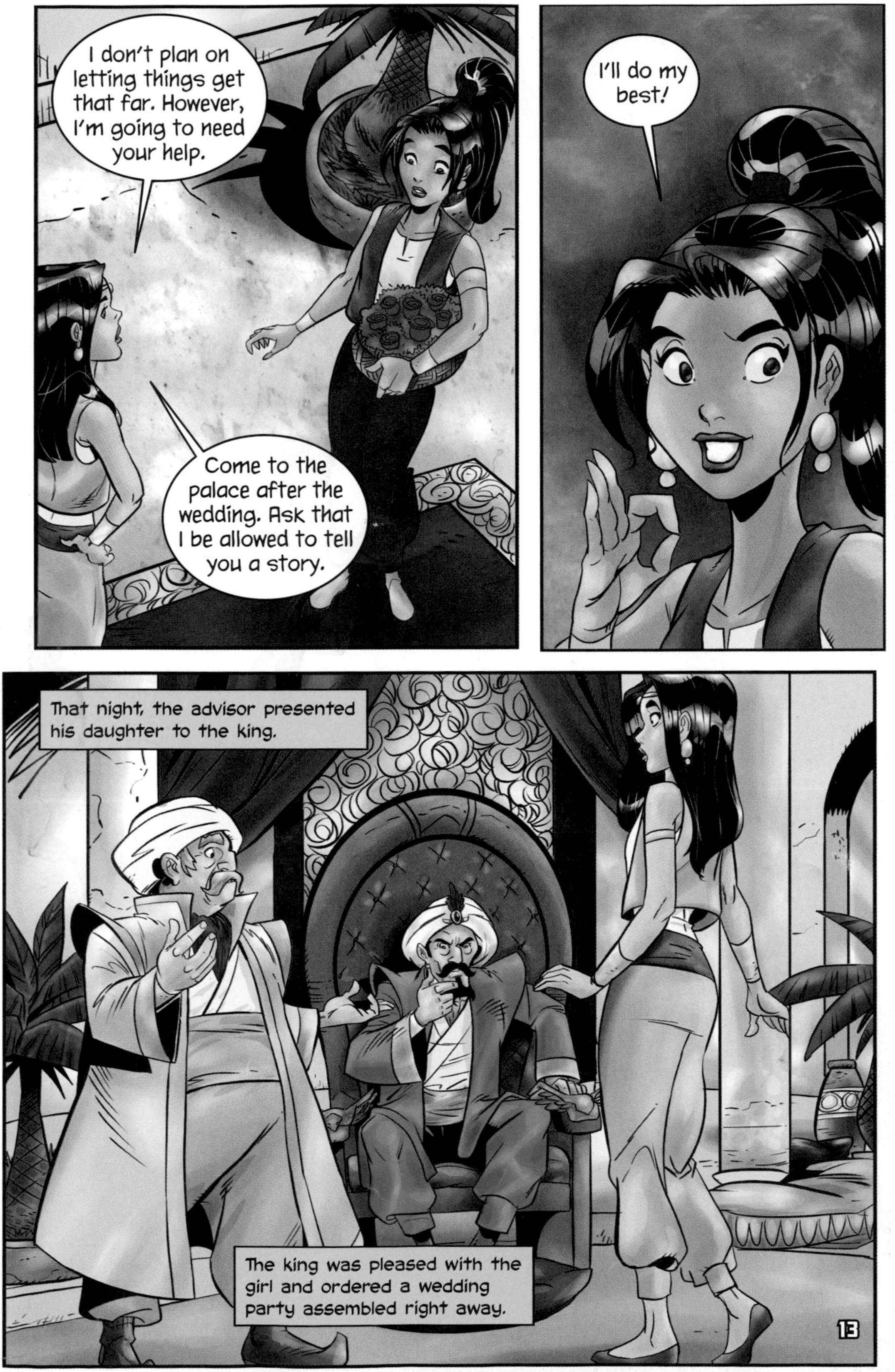
I don't plan on letting things get that far. However, I'm going to need your help.
Come to the palace after the wedding. Ask that I be allowed to tell you a story.
I'll do my best!
That night, the advisor presented his daughter to the king.
The king was pleased with the girl and ordered a wedding party assembled right away.

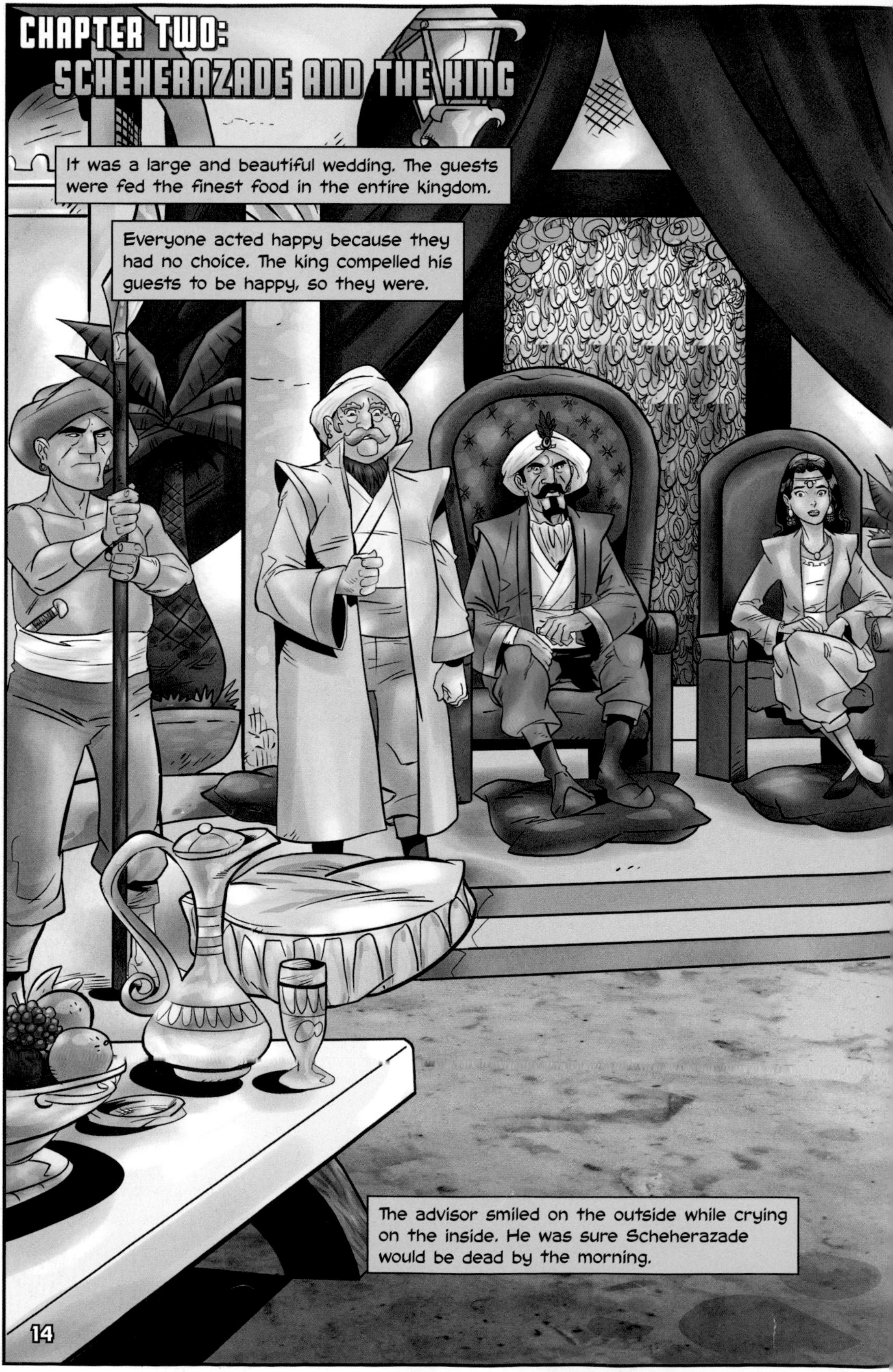
CHAPTER TWO:
SCHEHERAZADE AND THE KING
It was a large and beautiful wedding. The guests were fed the finest food in the entire kingdom.
Everyone acted happy because they had no choice. The king compelled his guests to be happy, so they were.
The advisor smiled on the outside while crying on the inside. He was sure Scheherazade would be dead by the morning.

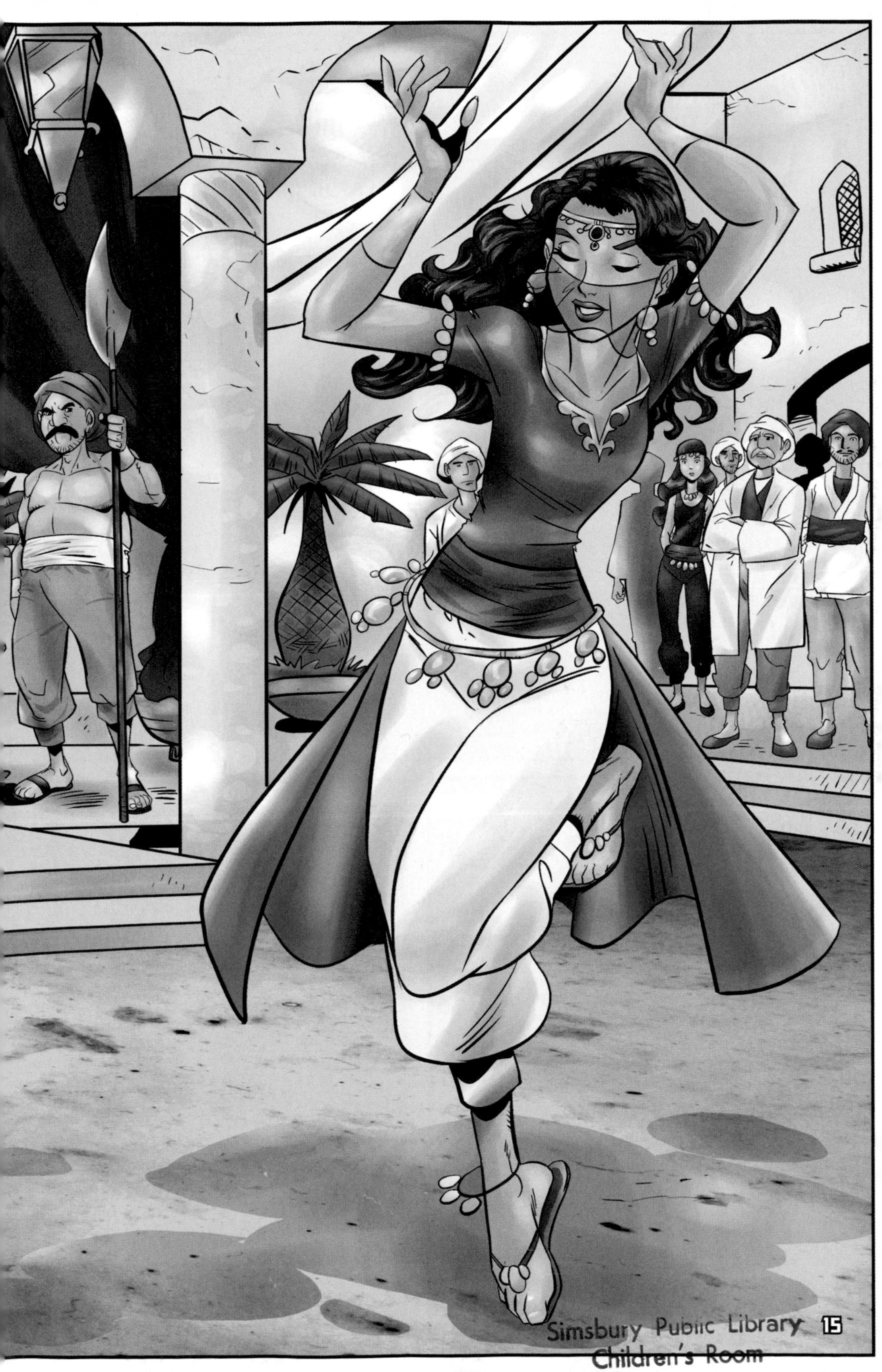

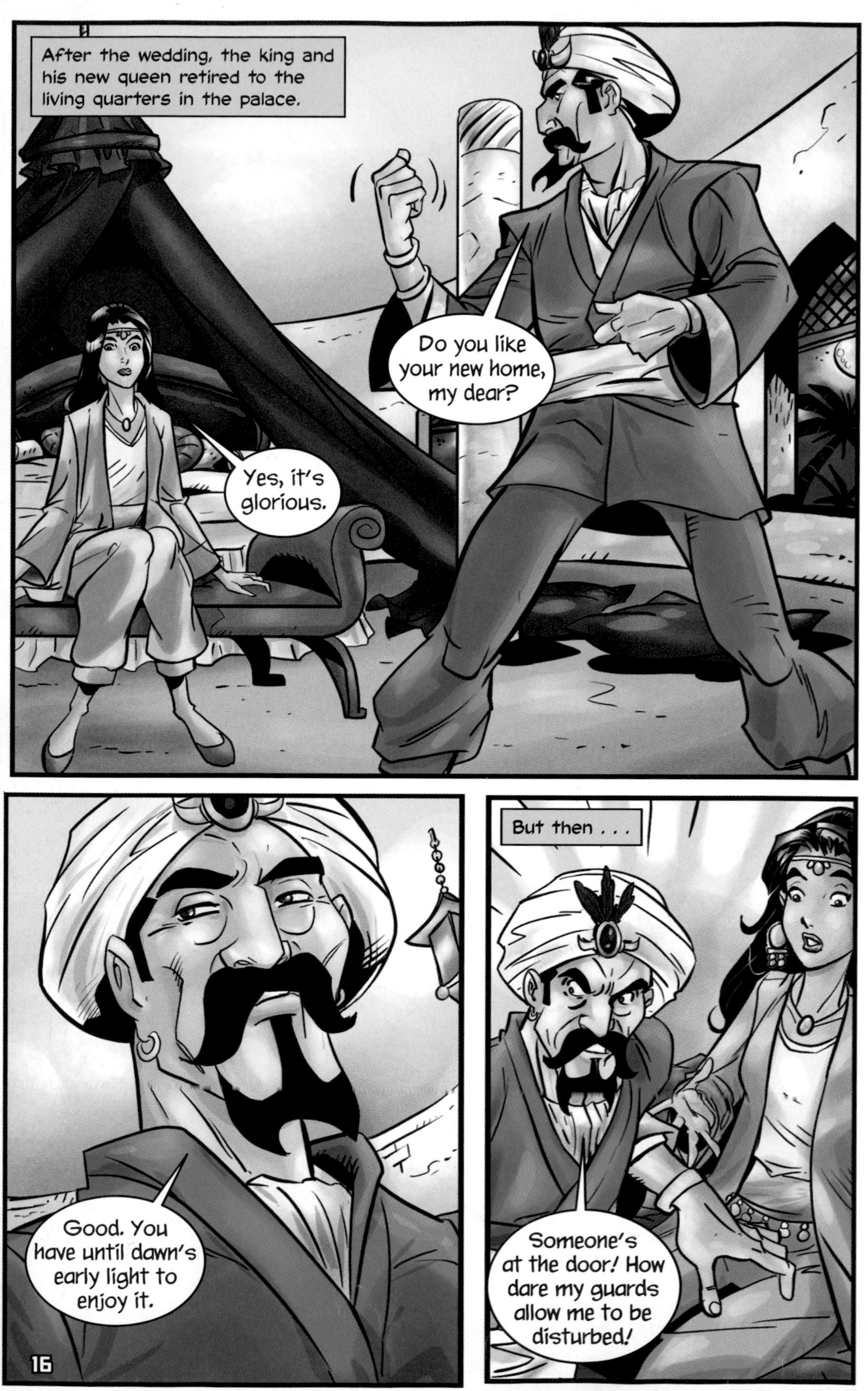

After the wedding, the king and his new queen retired to the living quarters in the palace.
Do you like your new home, my dear?
Yes, it's glorious.
Good. You have until dawn's early light to enjoy it.
But then . . .
Someone's at the door! How dare my guards allow me to be disturbed!

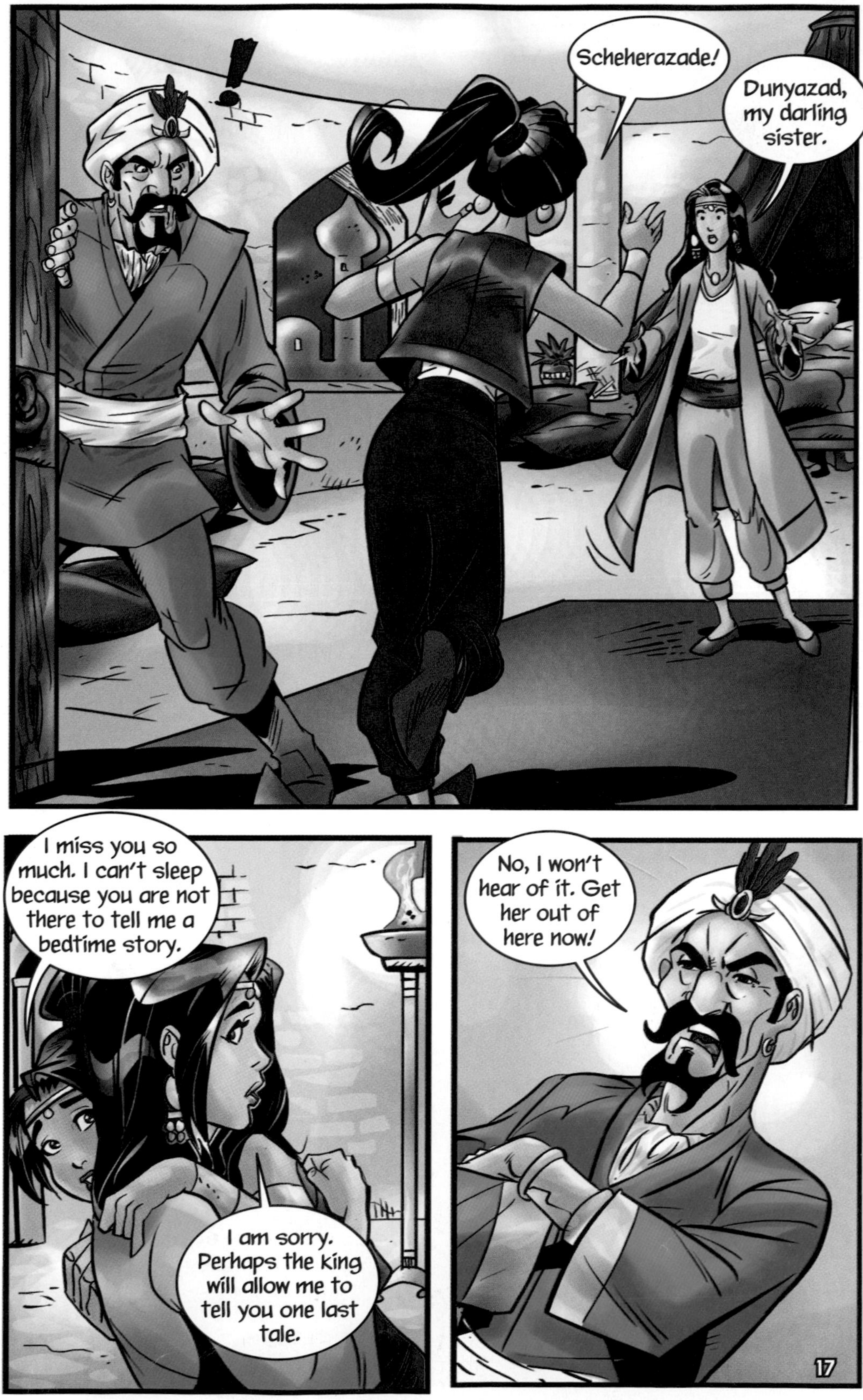
!
Scheherazade!
Dunyazad, my darling sister.
I miss you so much. I can't sleep because you are not there to tell me a bedtime story.
I am sorry. Perhaps the king will allow me to tell you one last tale.
No, I won't hear of it. Get her out of here now!

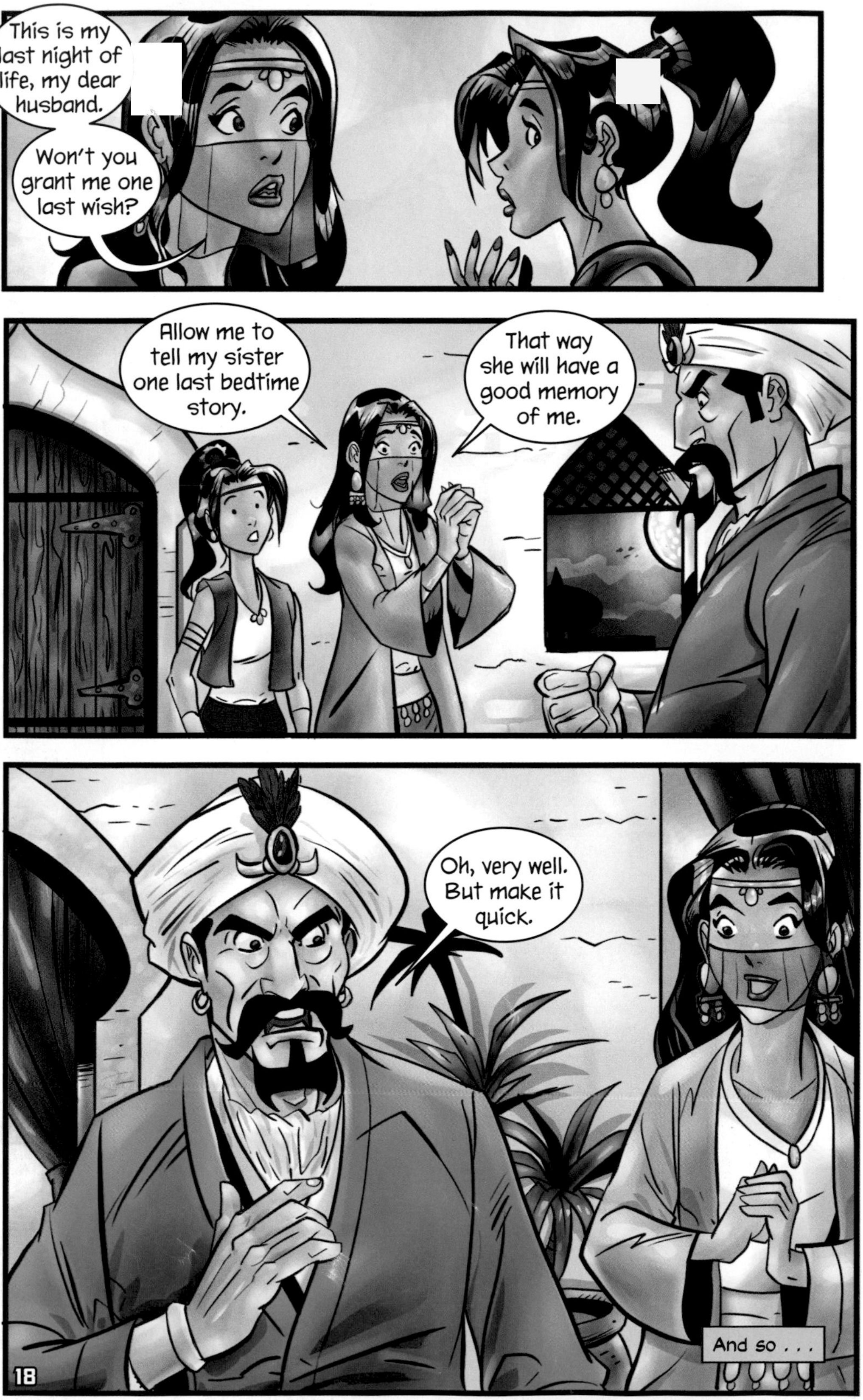
This is my last night of life, my dear husband.
Won't you grant me one last wish?
Allow me to tell my sister one last bedtime story.
That way she will have a good memory of me.
Oh, very well. But make it quick.
And so . . .

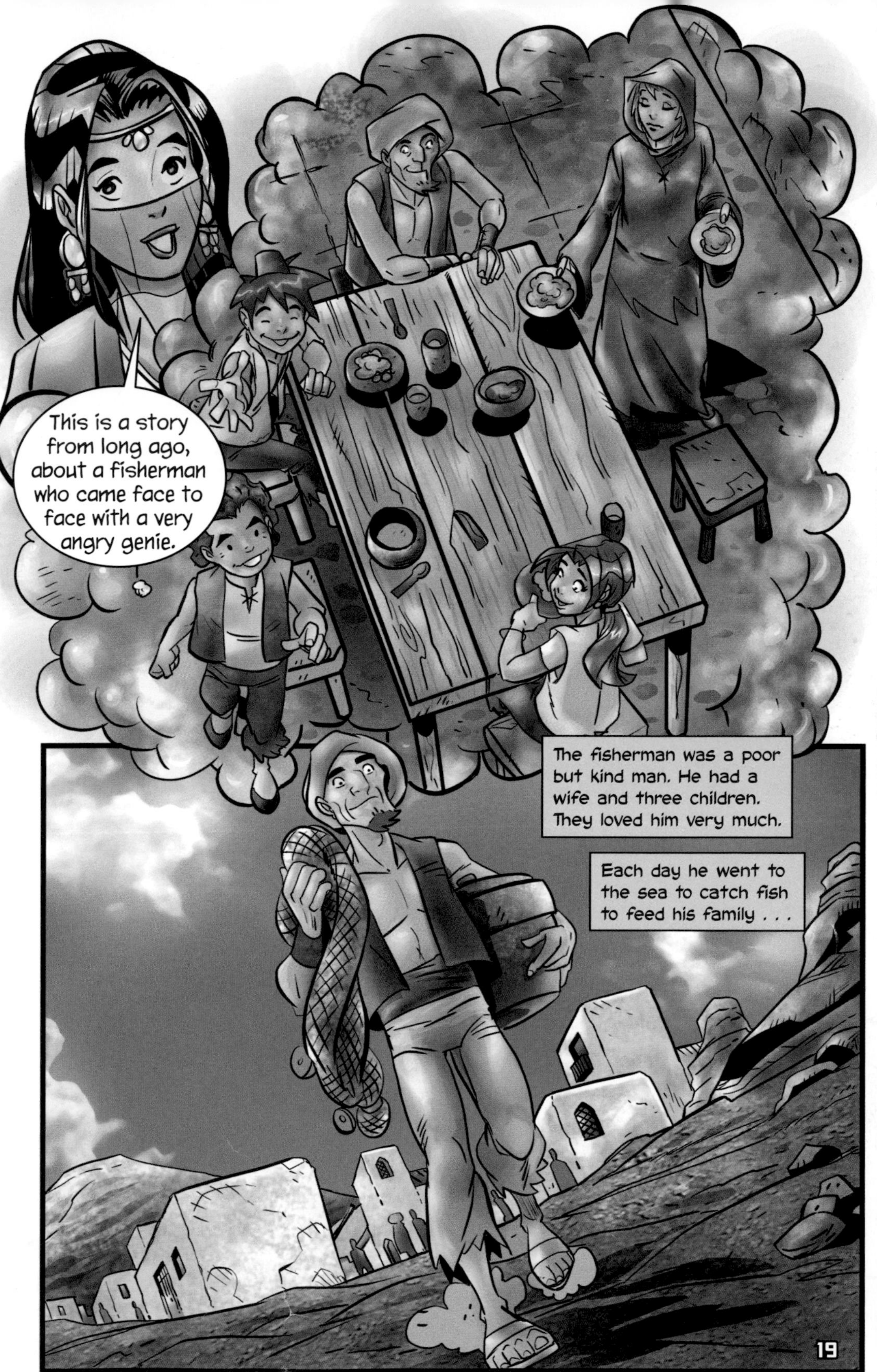

This is a story from long ago, about a fisherman who came face to face with a very angry genie.
The fisherman was a poor but kind man. He had a wife and three children. They loved him very much.
Each day he went to the sea to catch fish to feed his family . . .

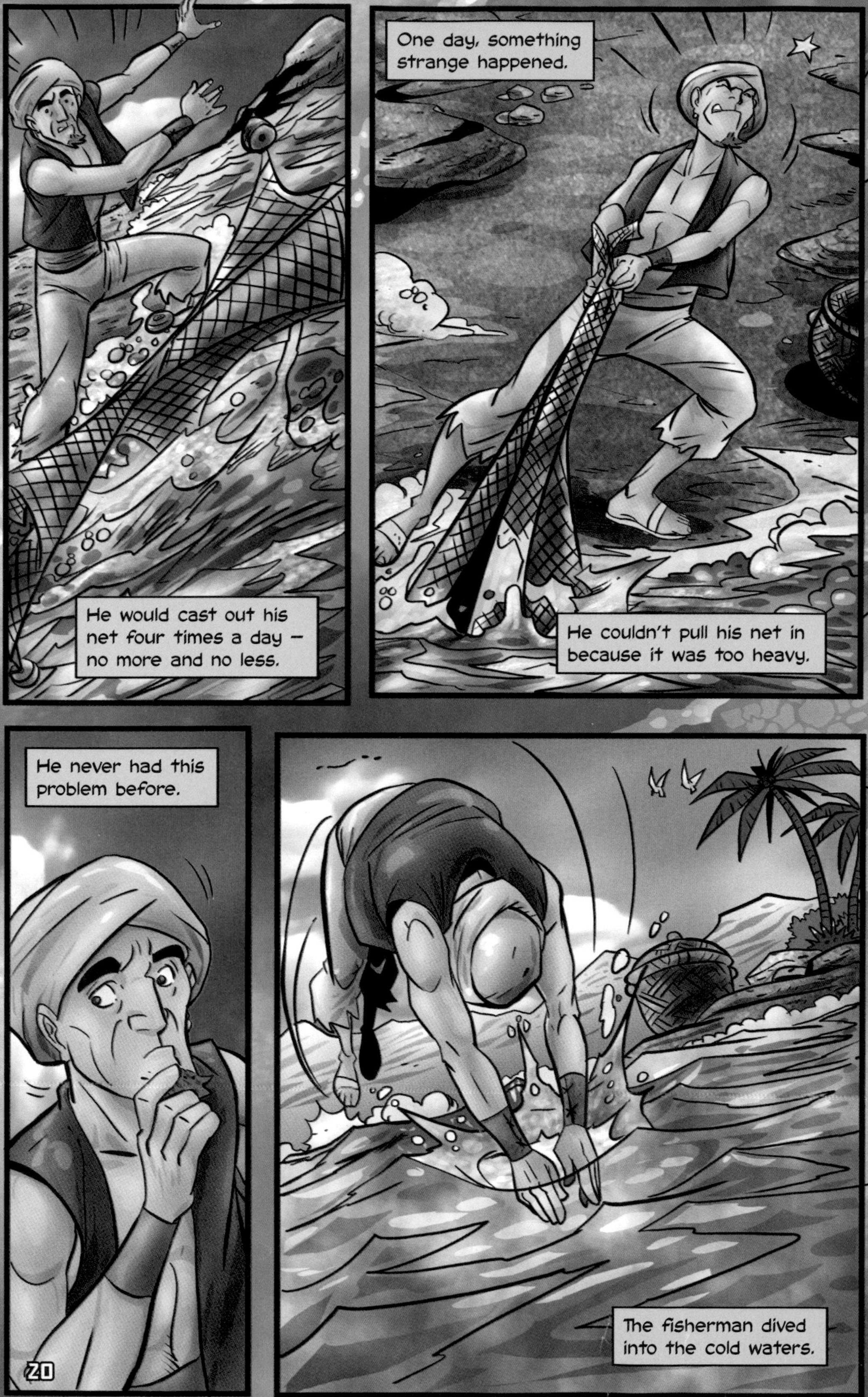
He would cast out his net four times a day — no more and no less.
One day, something strange happened.
He couldn't pull his net in because it was too heavy.
He never had this problem before.
The fisherman dived into the cold waters.

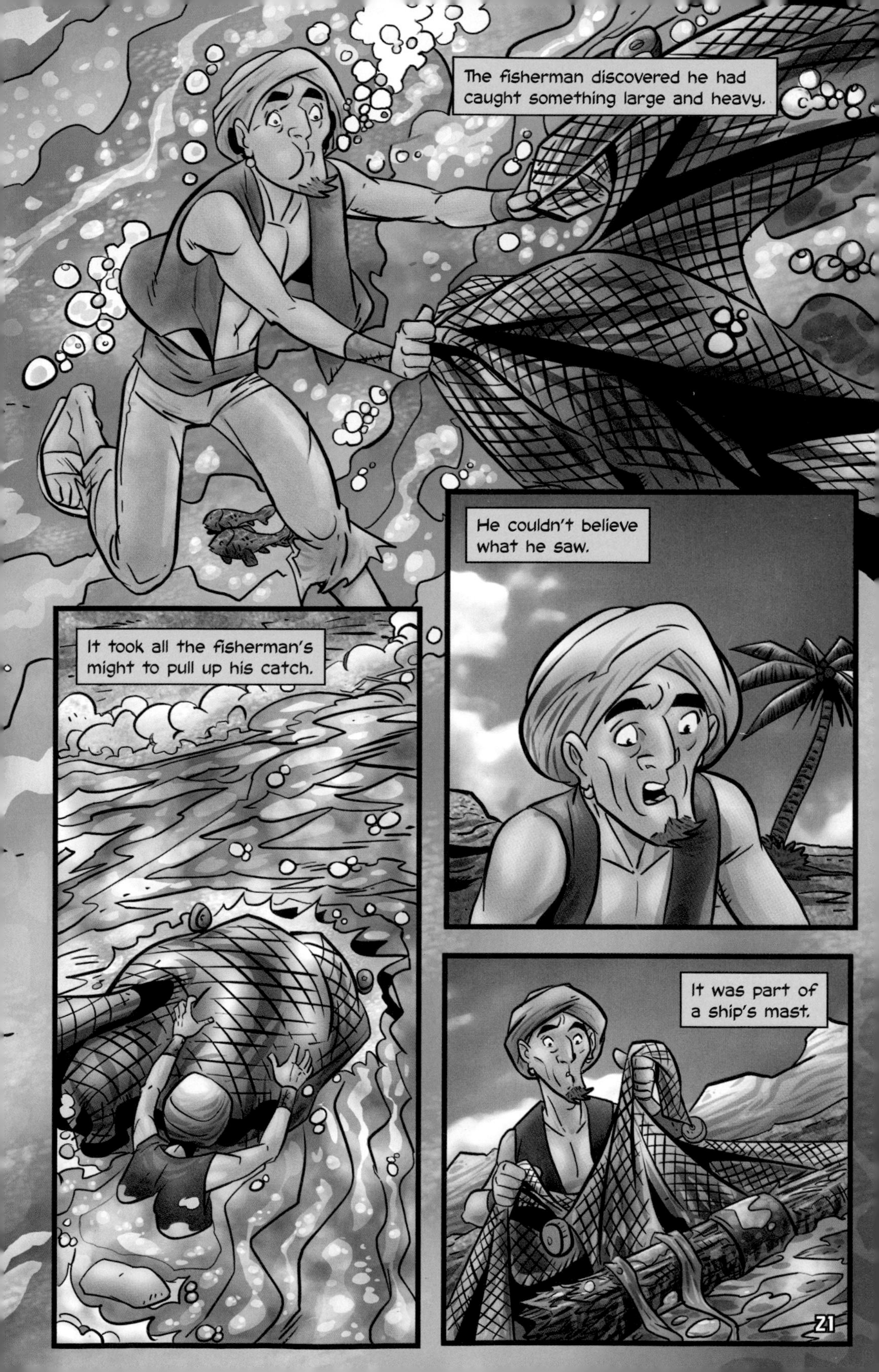
The fisherman discovered he had caught something large and heavy.
It took all the fisherman's might to pull up his catch.
He couldn't believe what he saw.
It was part of a ship's mast.

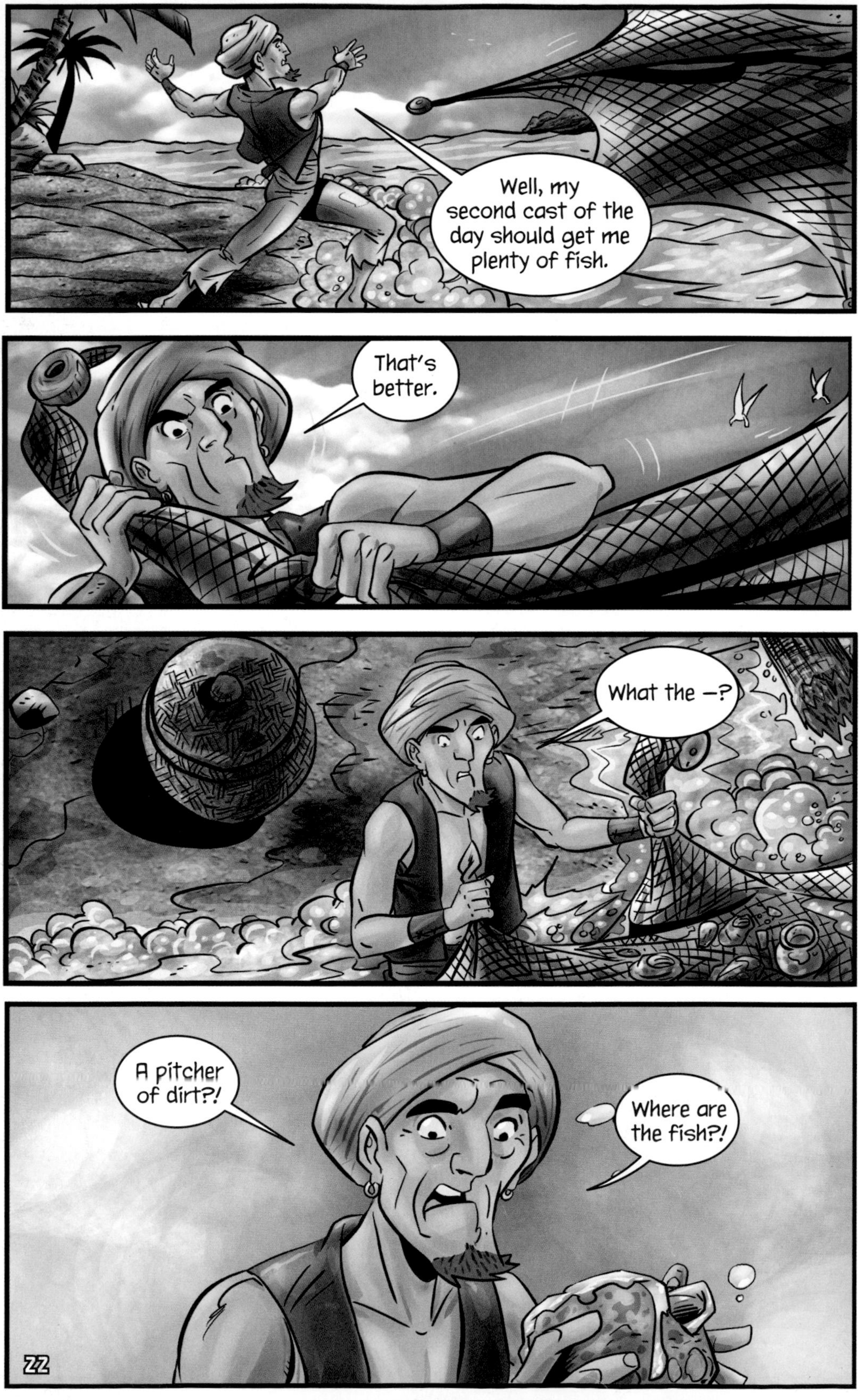
Well, my second cast of the day should get me plenty of fish.
That's better.
What the –?
A pitcher of dirt?!
Where are the fish?!

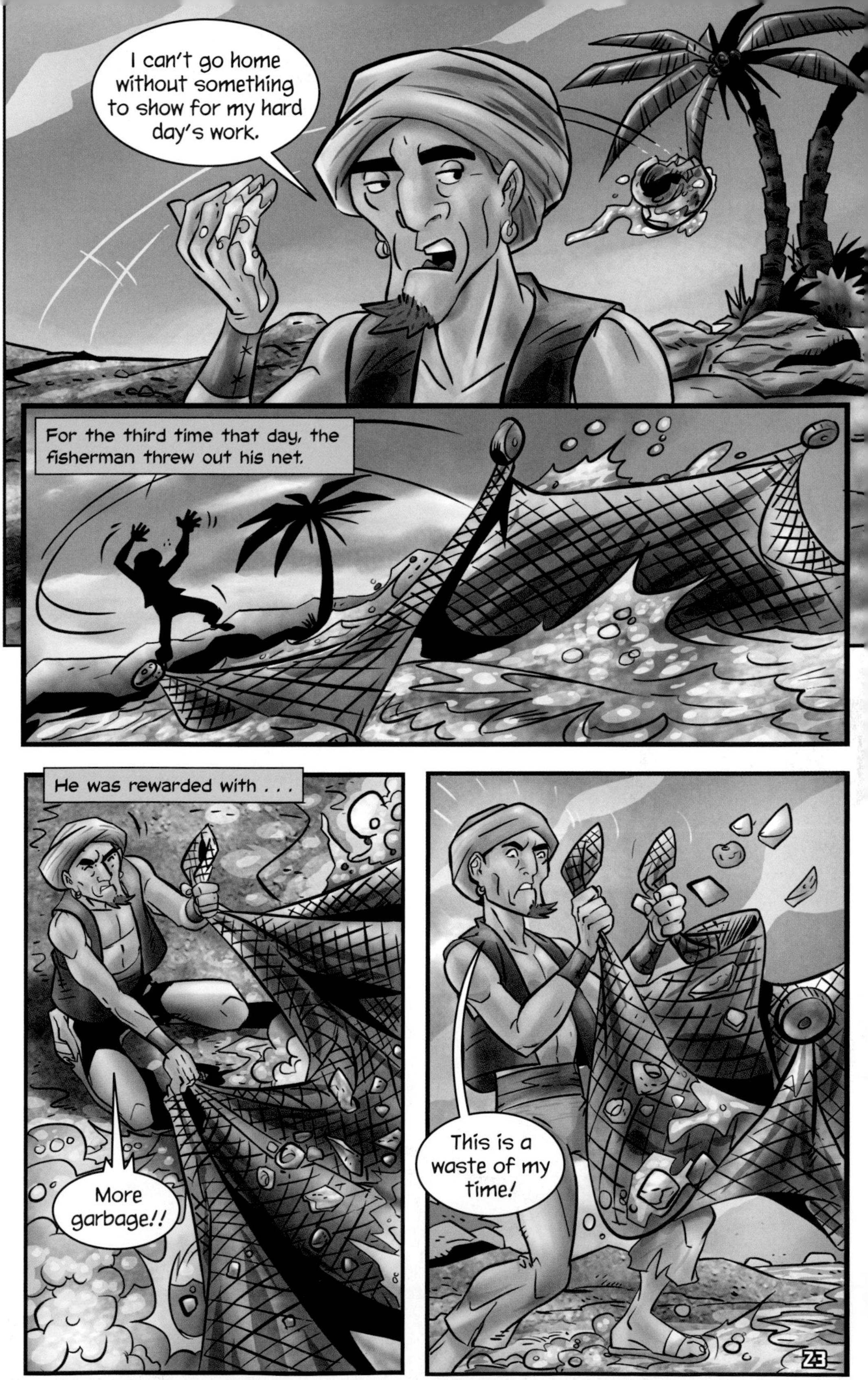
I can't go home without something to show for my hard day's work.
For the third time that day, the fisherman threw out his net.
He was rewarded with . . .
More garbage!!
This is a waste of my time!

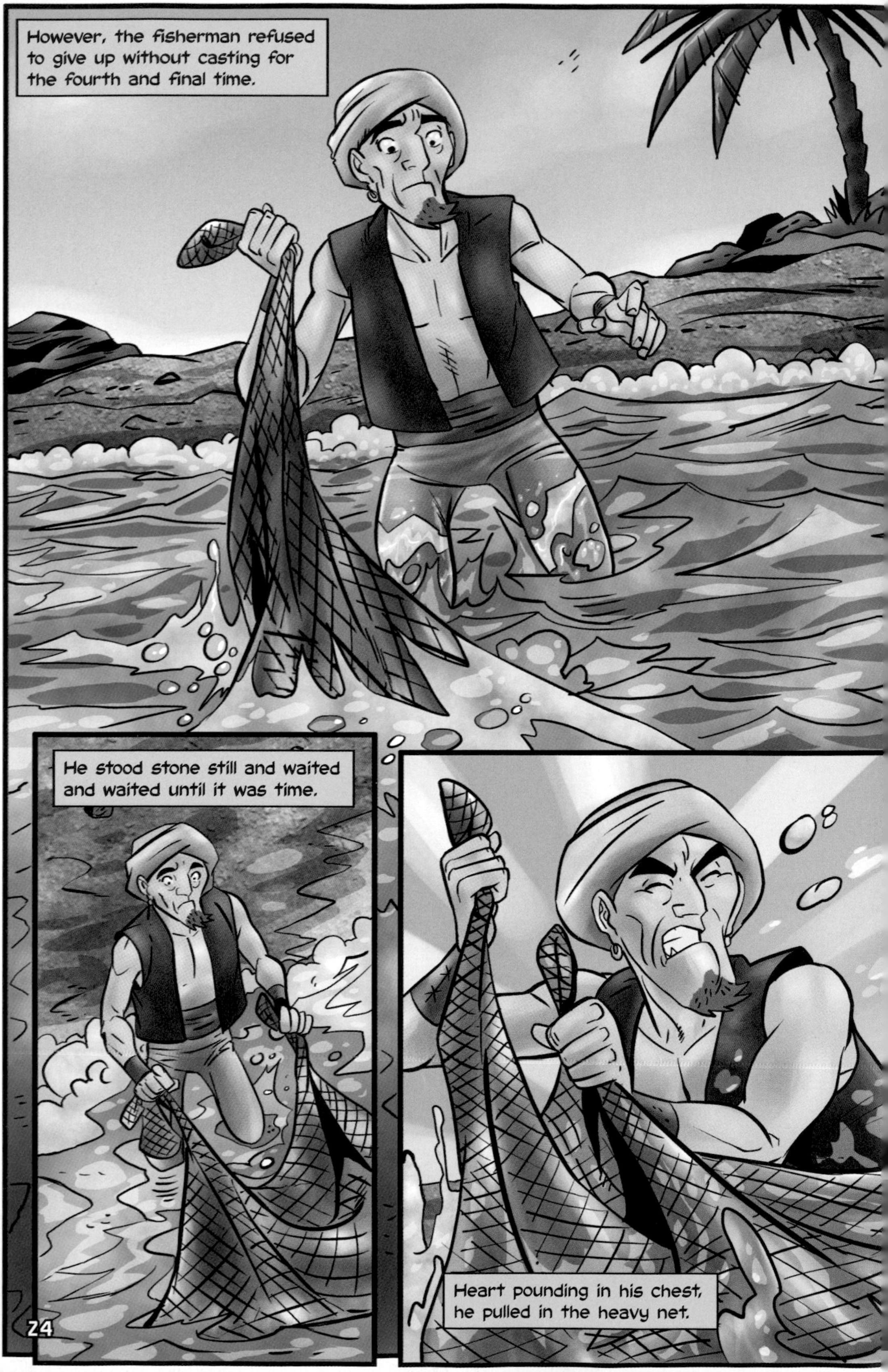
However, the fisherman refused to give up without casting for the fourth and final time.
He stood stone still and waited and waited until it was time.
Heart pounding in his chest, he pulled in the heavy net.

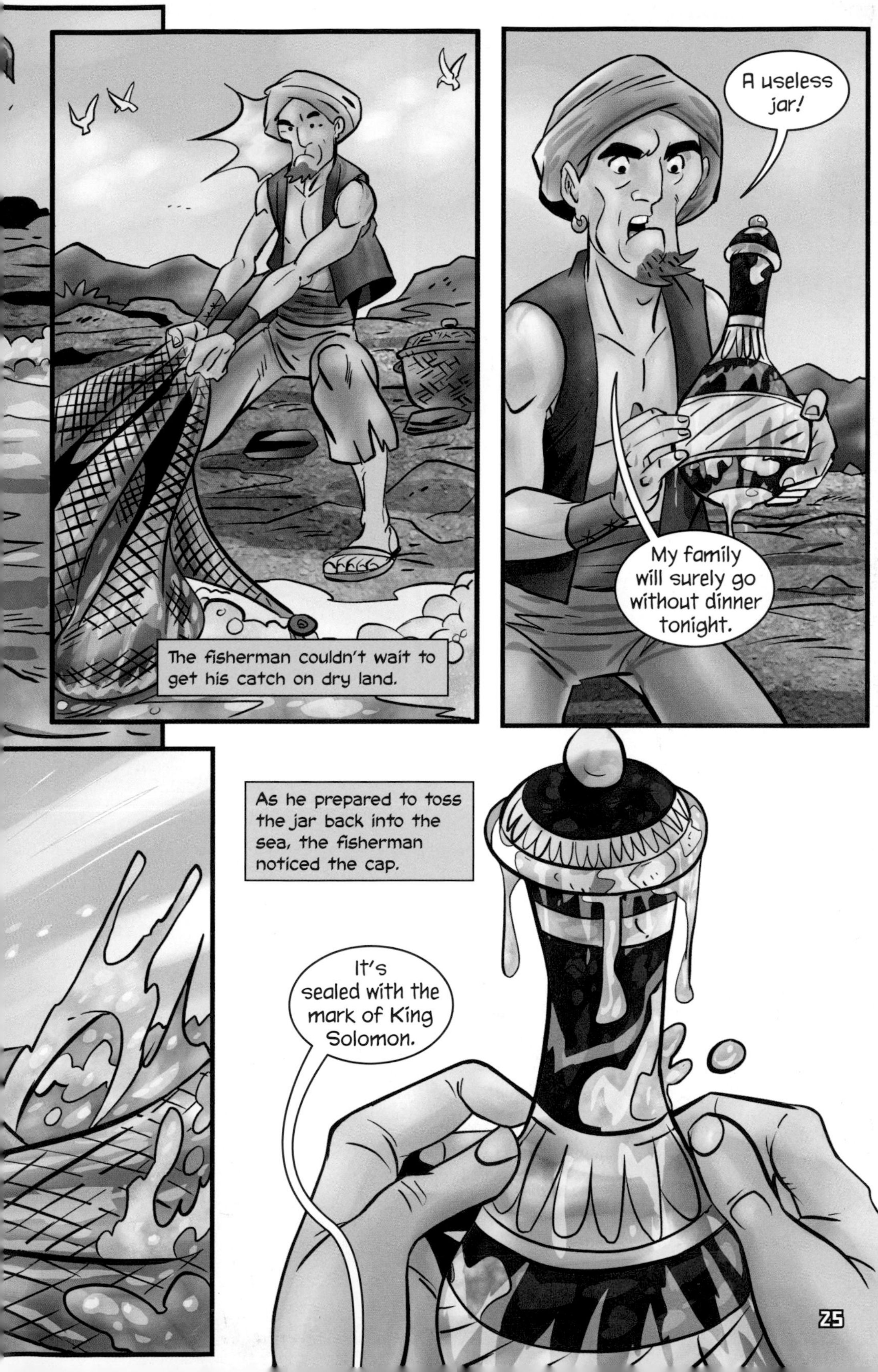

The fisherman couldn't wait to get his catch on dry land.
A useless jar!
My family will surely go without dinner tonight.
As he prepared to toss the jar back into the sea, the fisherman noticed the cap.
It's sealed with the mark of King Solomon.

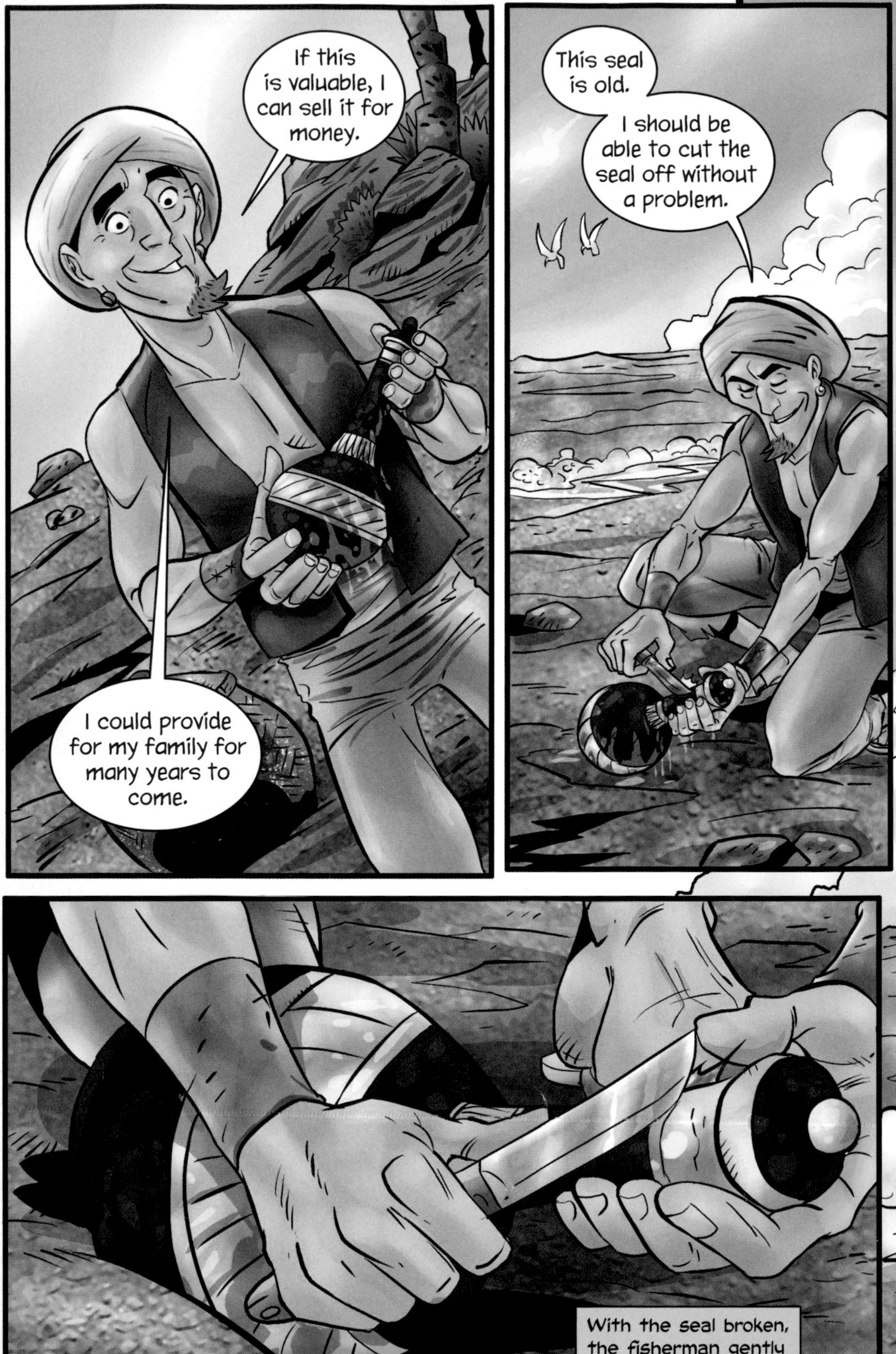
If this is valuable, I can sell it for money.
I could provide for my family for many years to come.
This seal is old.
I should be able to cut the seal off without a problem.
With the seal broken, the fisherman gently removed the cap.

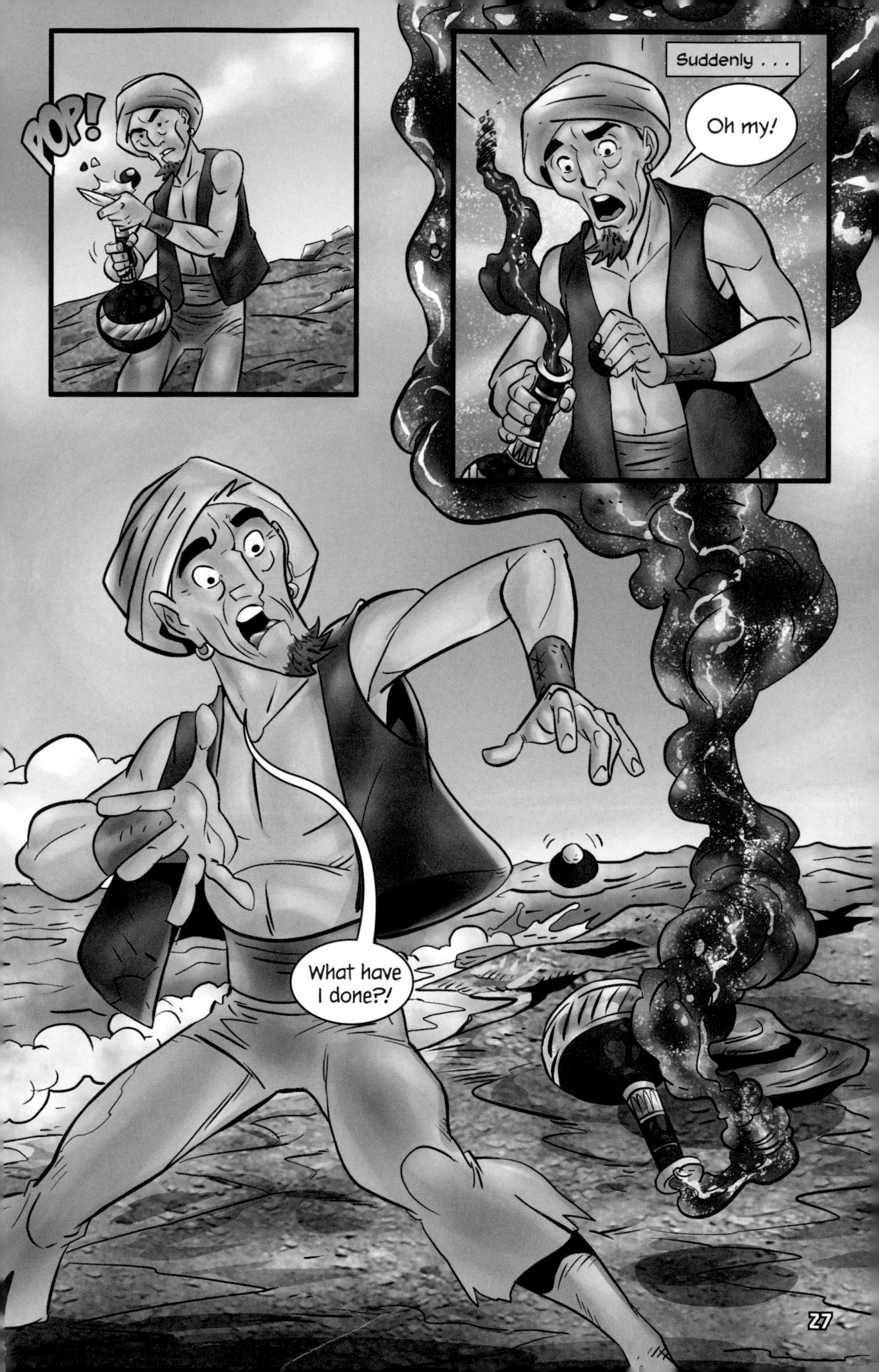
POP!
Suddenly . . .
Oh my!
What have I done?!

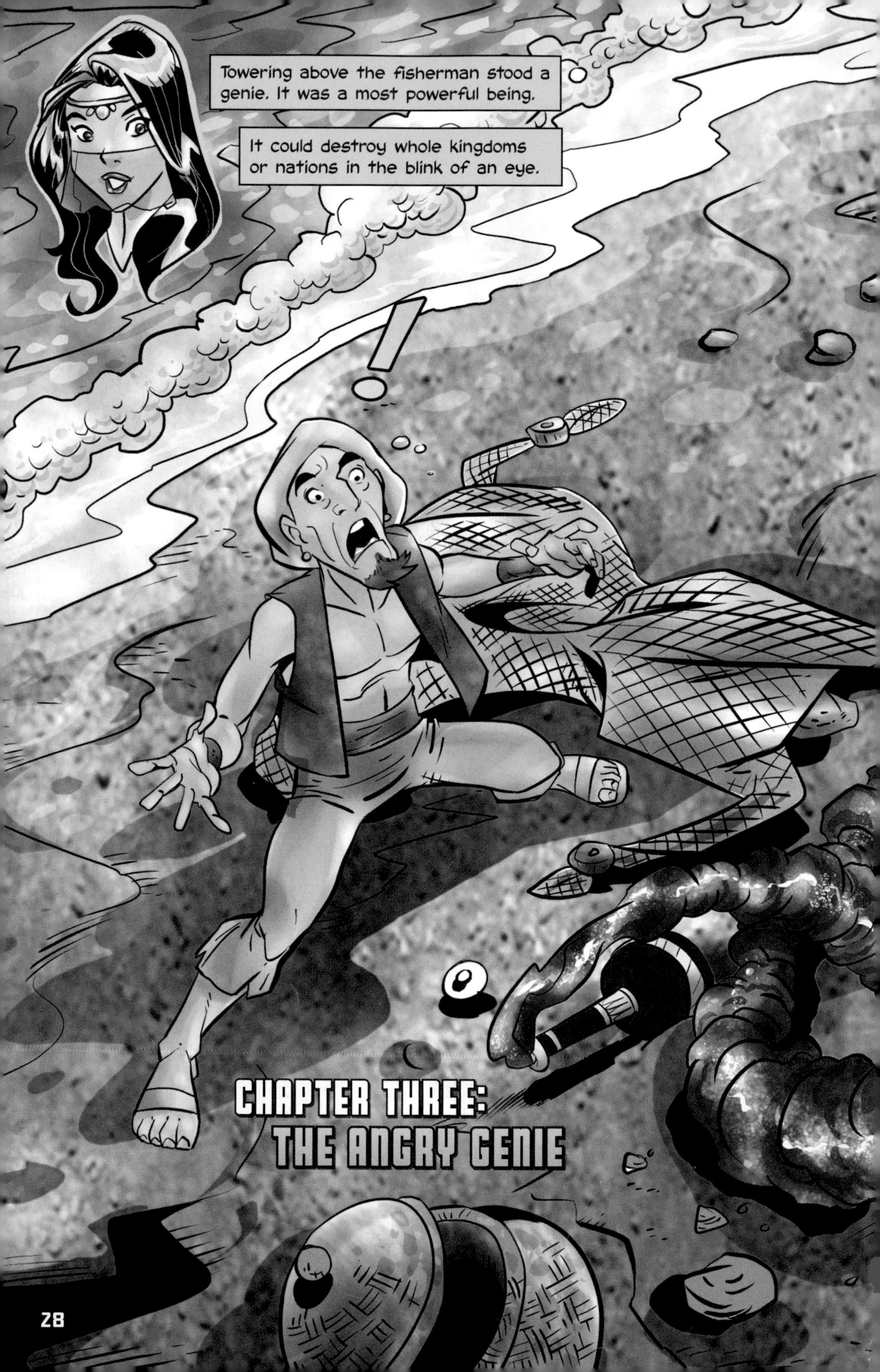
Towering above the fisherman stood a genie. It was a most powerful being.
It could destroy whole kingdoms or nations in the blink of an eye.
!
CHAPTER THREE:
THE ANGRY GENIE

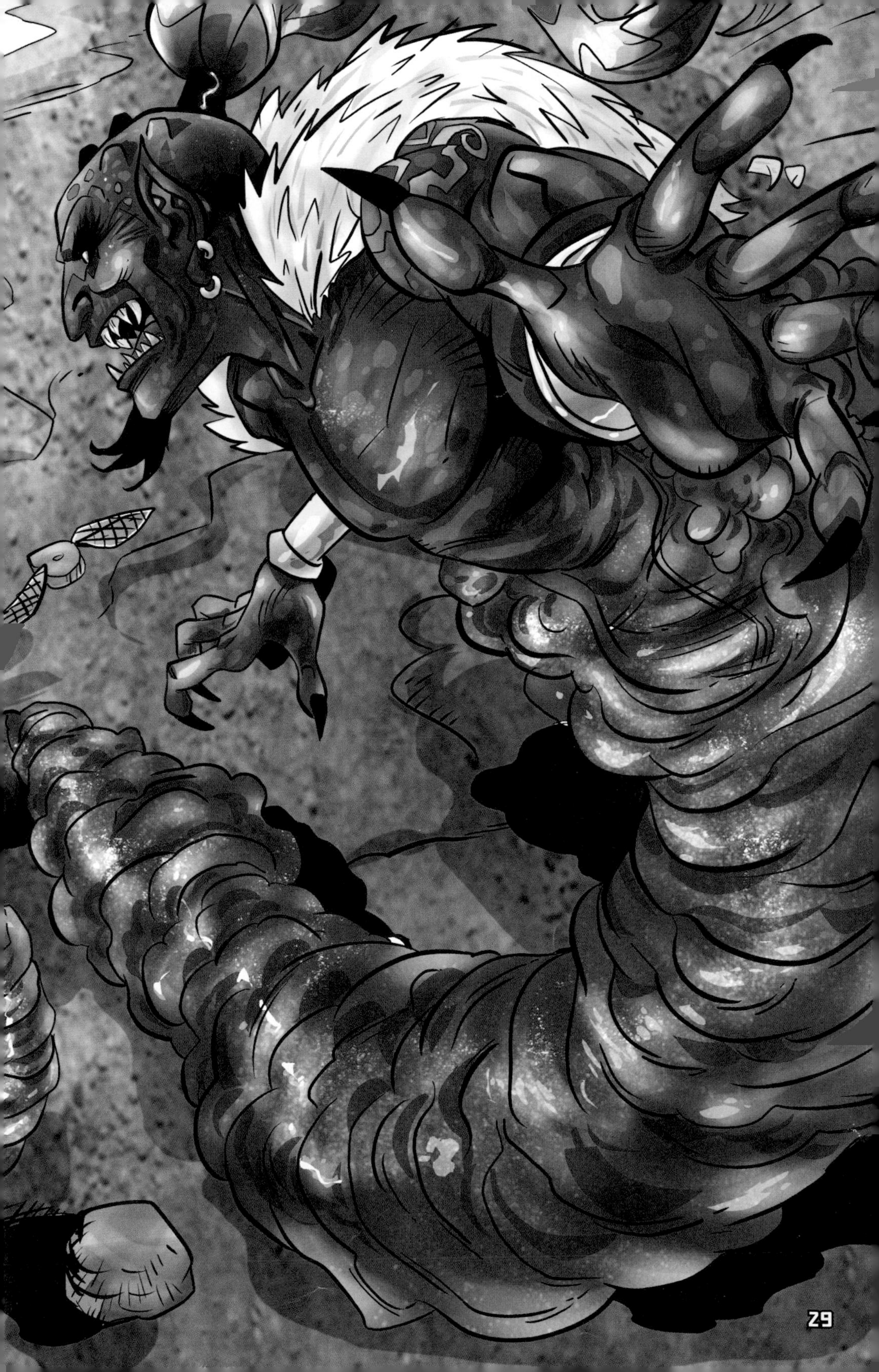

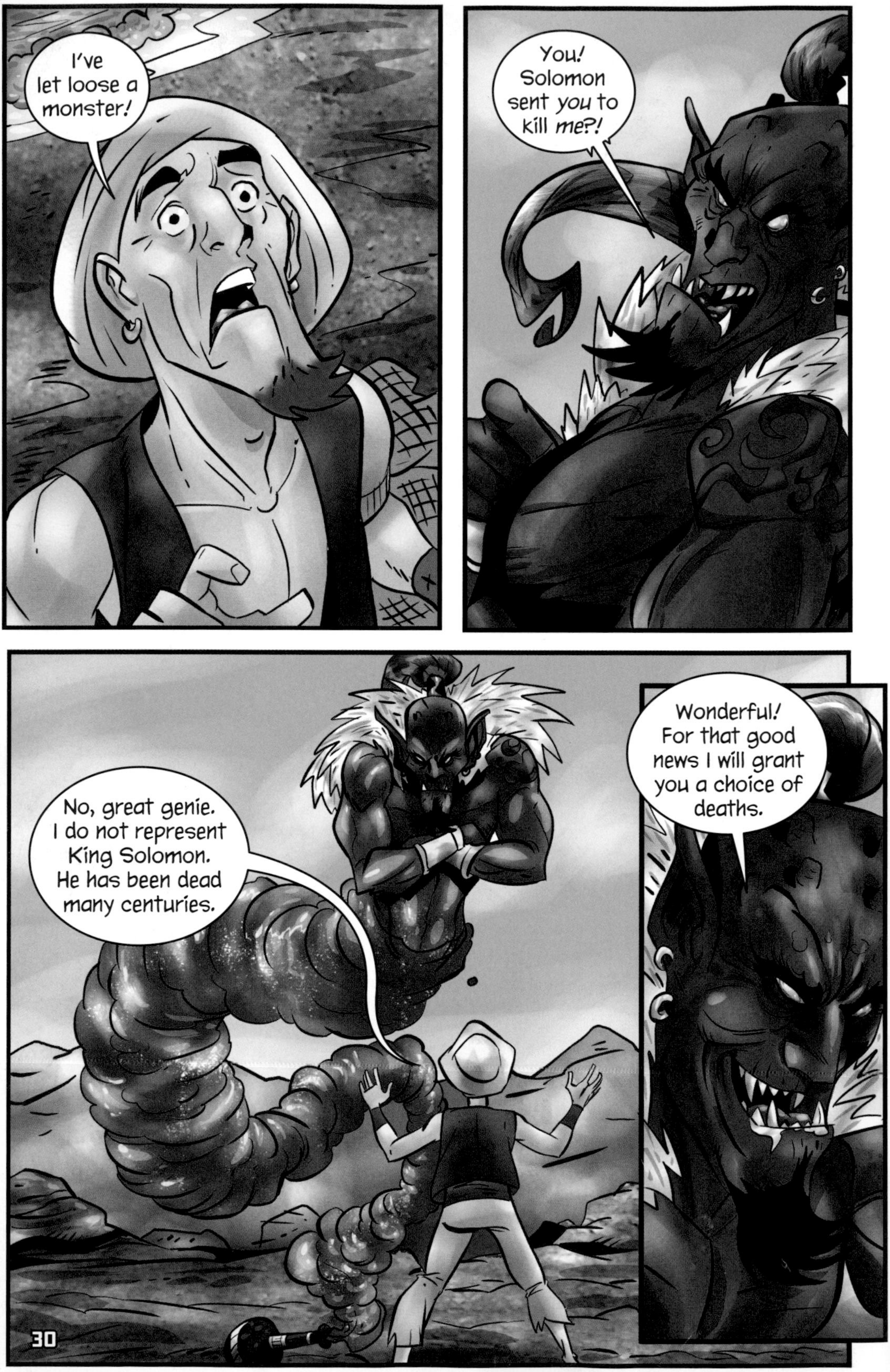
I've let loose a monster!
You! Solomon sent *you* to kill *me*?!
No, great genie. I do not represent King Solomon. He has been dead many centuries.
Wonderful! For that good news I will grant you a choice of deaths.

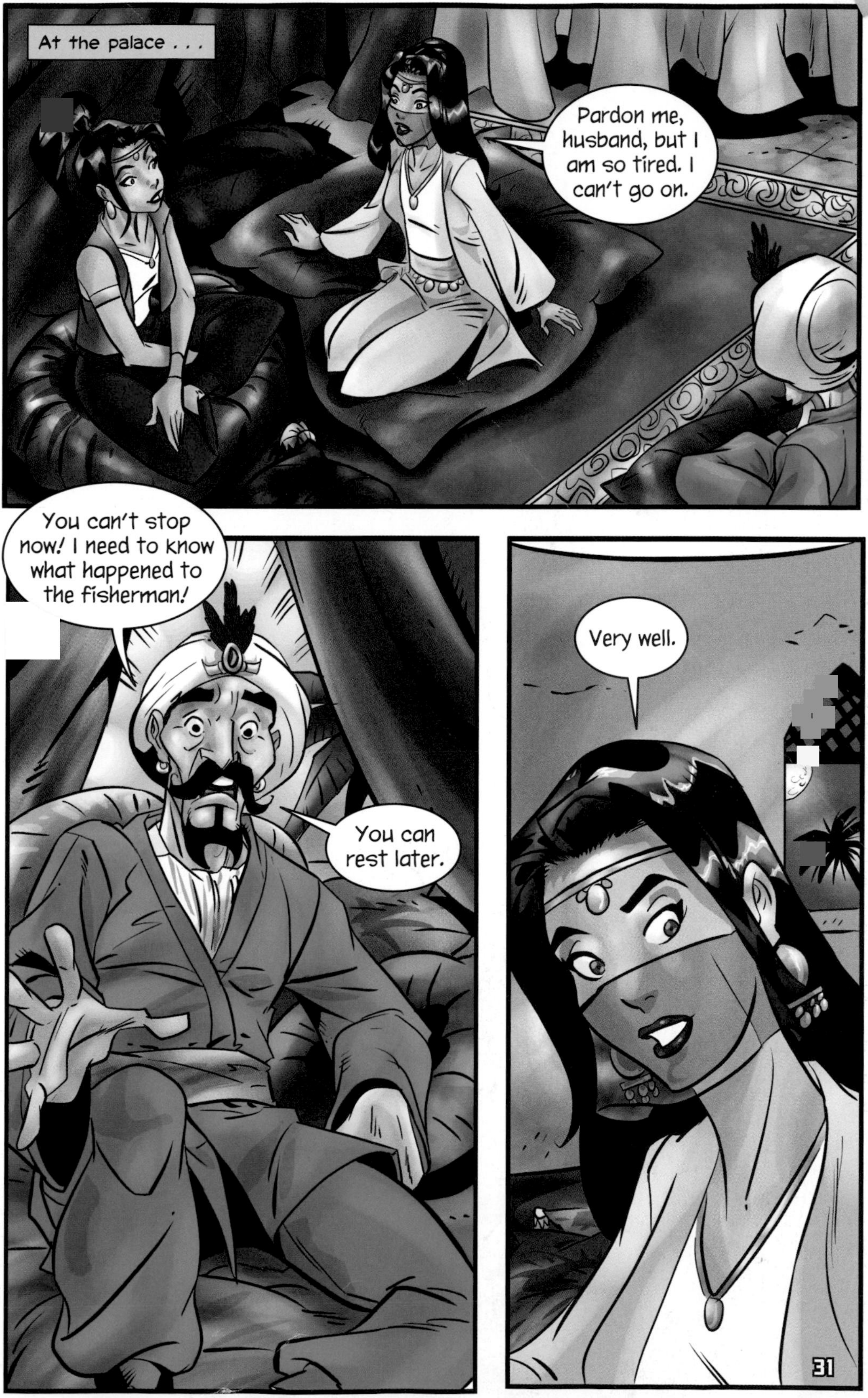
At the palace . . .
Pardon me, husband, but I am so tired. I can't go on.
You can't stop now! I need to know what happened to the fisherman!
You can rest later.
Very well.

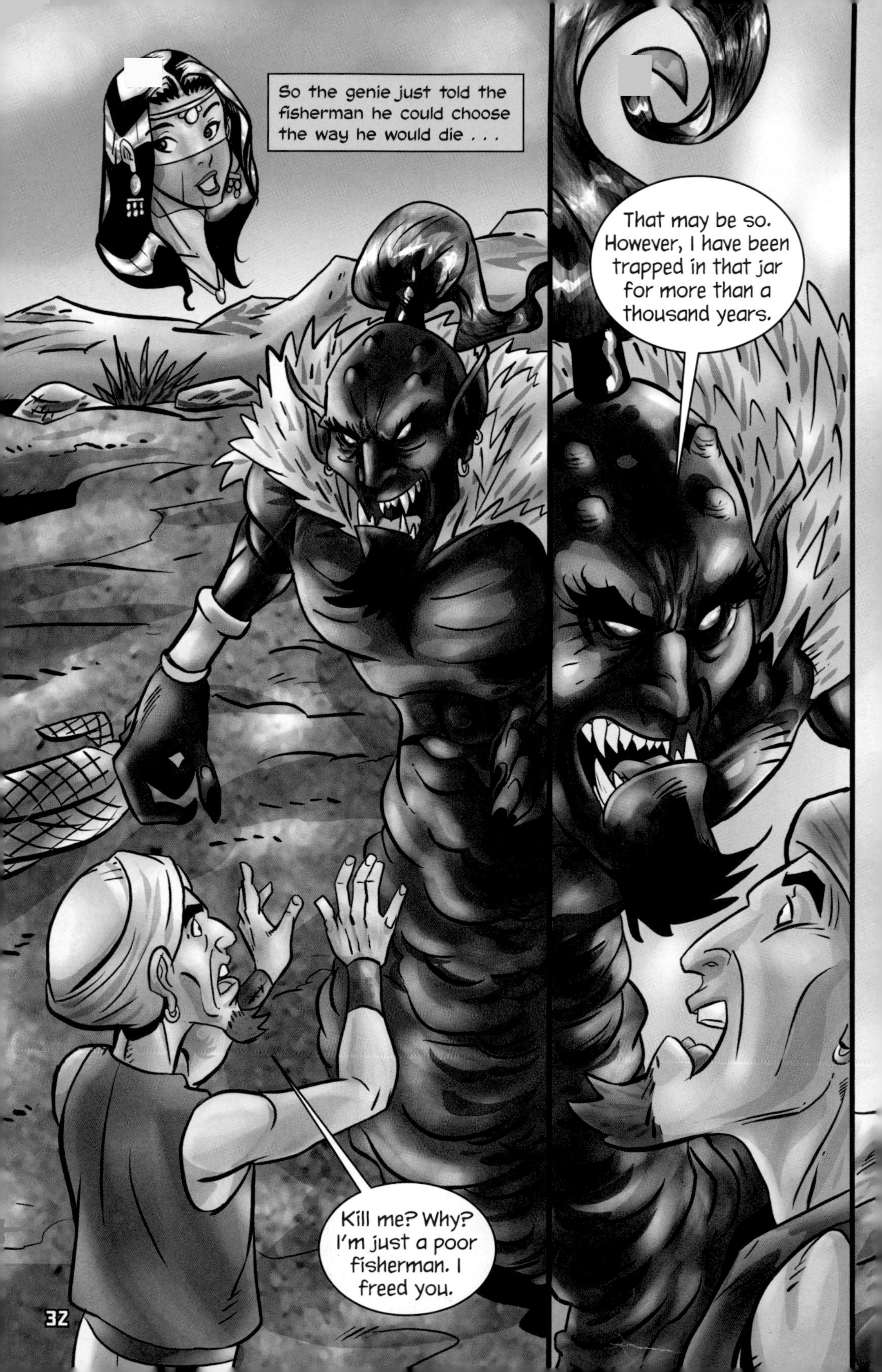
So the genie just told the fisherman he could choose the way he would die . . .
Kill me? Why? I'm just a poor fisherman. I freed you.
That may be so. However, I have been trapped in that jar for more than a thousand years.

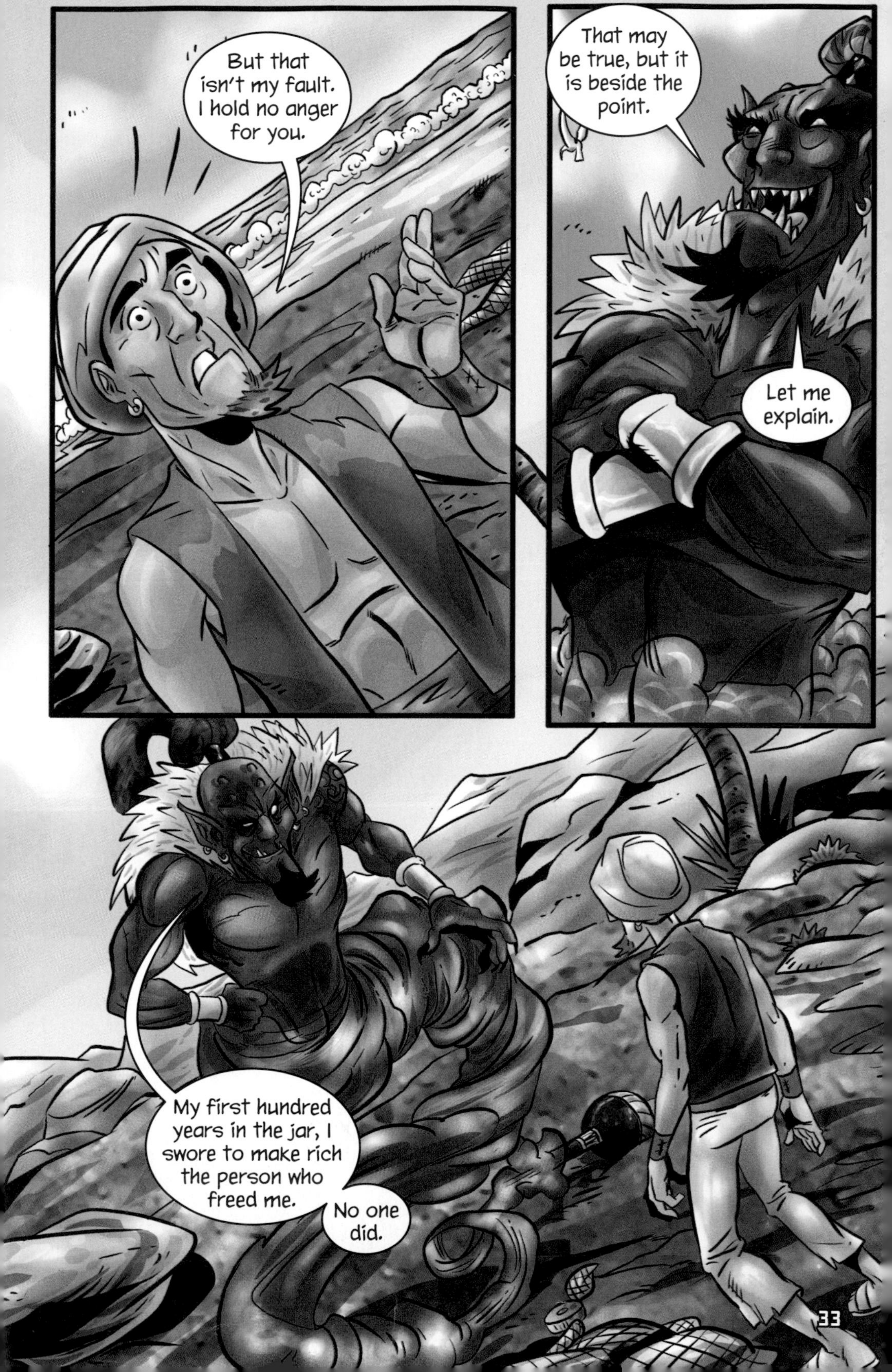
But that isn't my fault. I hold no anger for you.
That may be true, but it is beside the point.
Let me explain.
My first hundred years in the jar, I swore to make rich the person who freed me.
No one did.

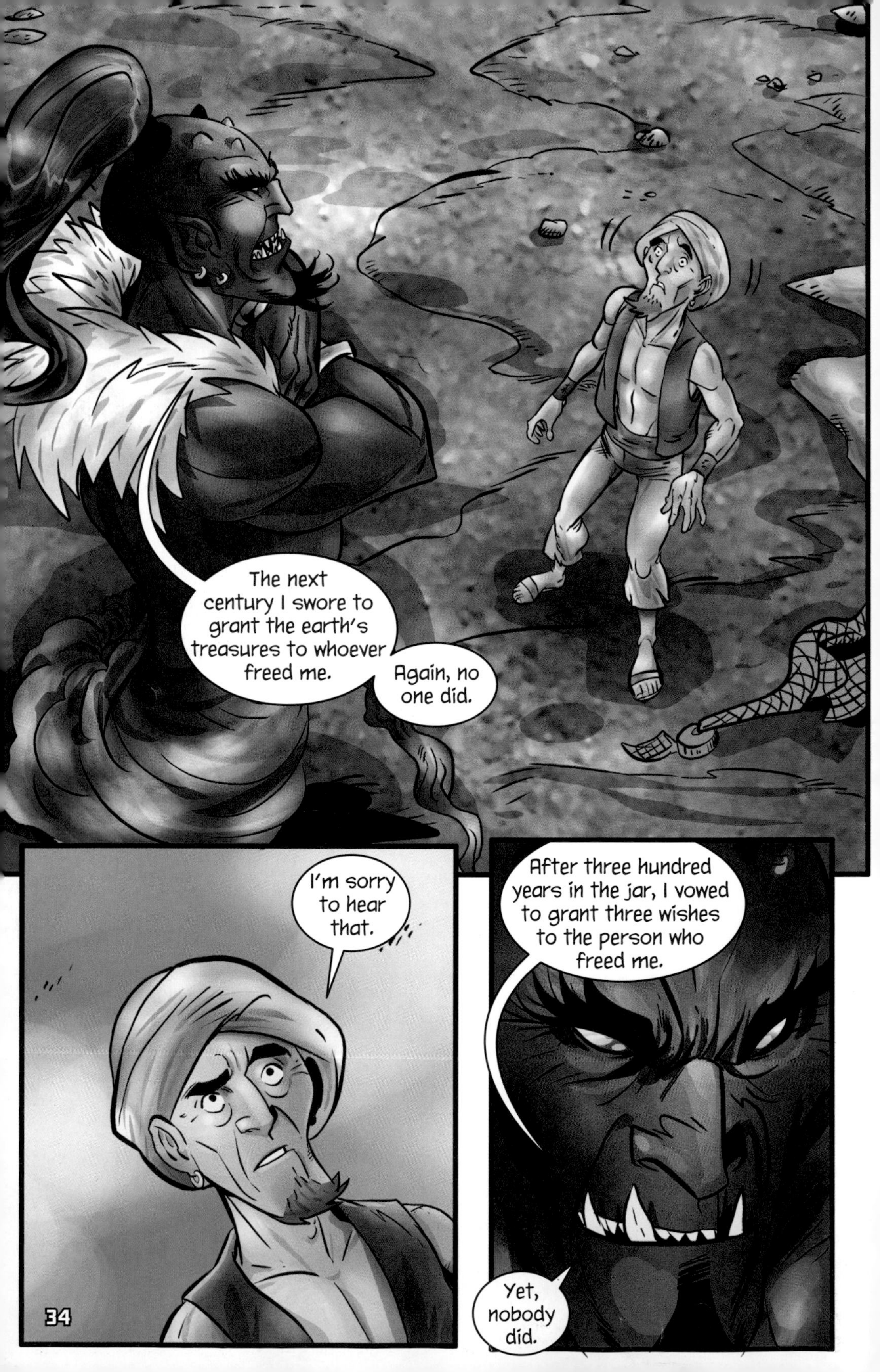
The next century I swore to grant the earth's treasures to whoever freed me.
Again, no one did.
I'm sorry to hear that.
After three hundred years in the jar, I vowed to grant three wishes to the person who freed me.
Yet, nobody did.

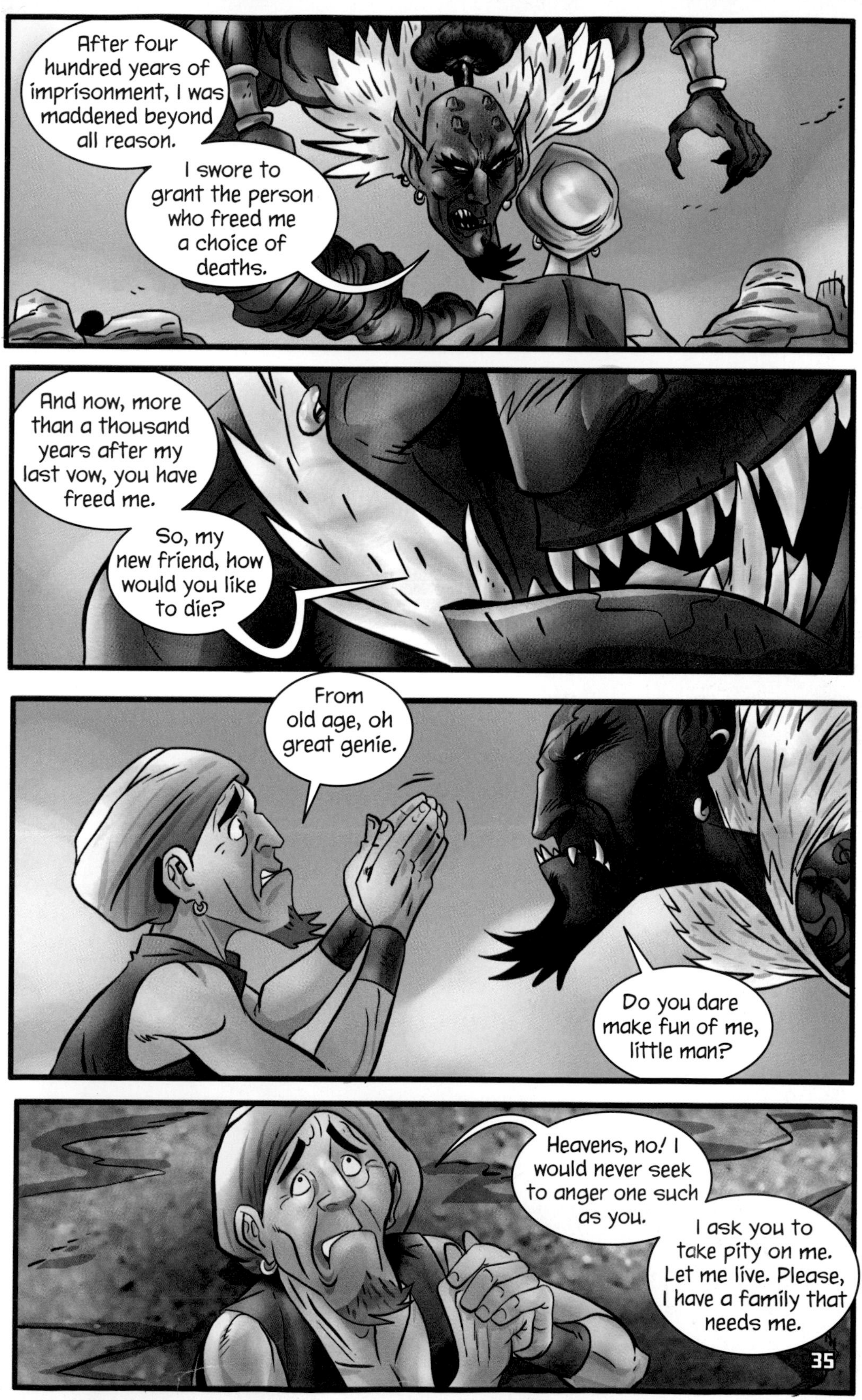
After four hundred years of imprisonment, I was maddened beyond all reason.
I swore to grant the person who freed me a choice of deaths.
And now, more than a thousand years after my last vow, you have freed me.
So, my new friend, how would you like to die?
From old age, oh great genie.
Do you dare make fun of me, little man?
Heavens, no! I would never seek to anger one such as you.
I ask you to take pity on me. Let me live. Please, I have a family that needs me.

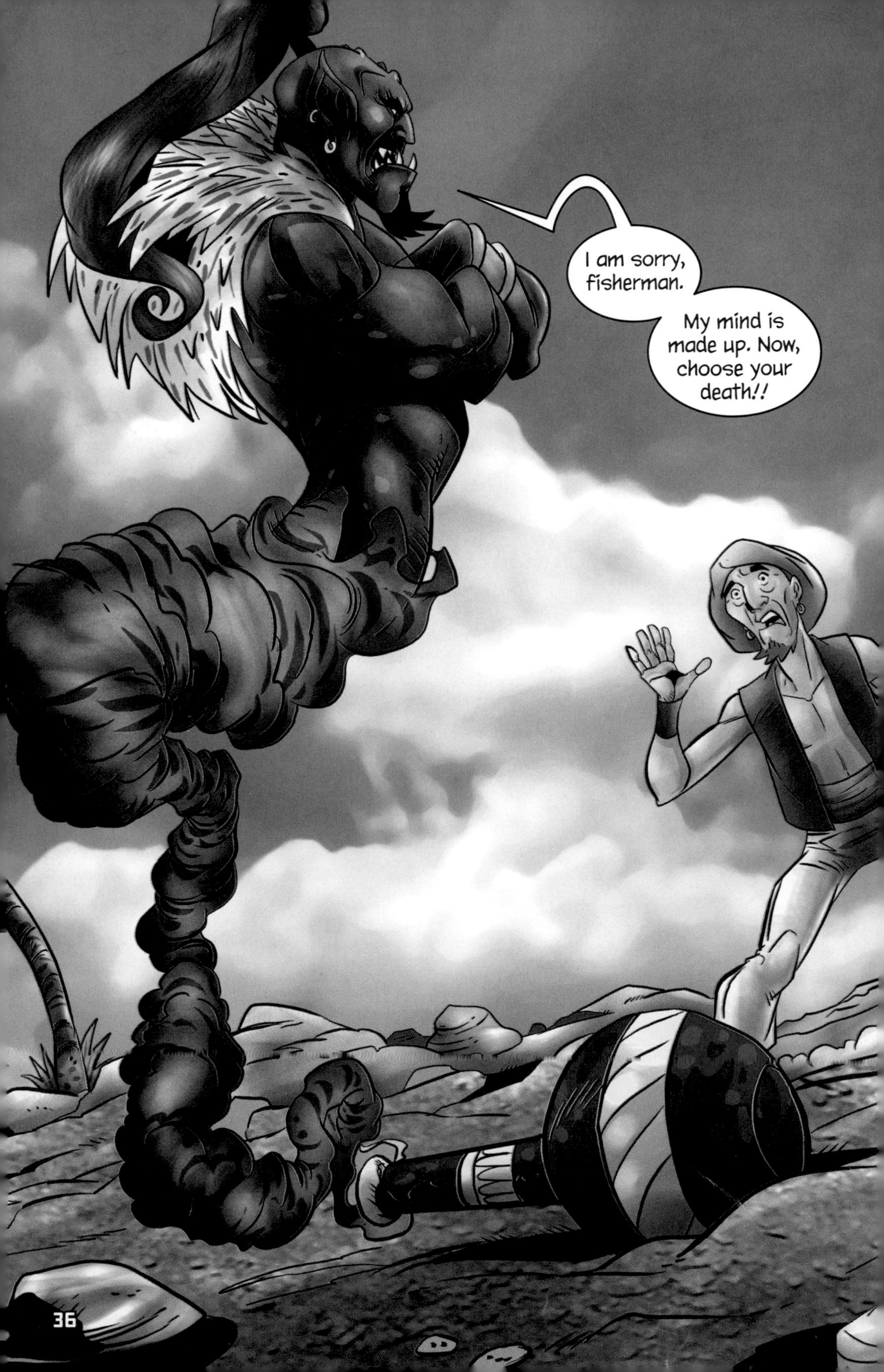
I am sorry, fisherman.
My mind is made up. Now, choose your death!!

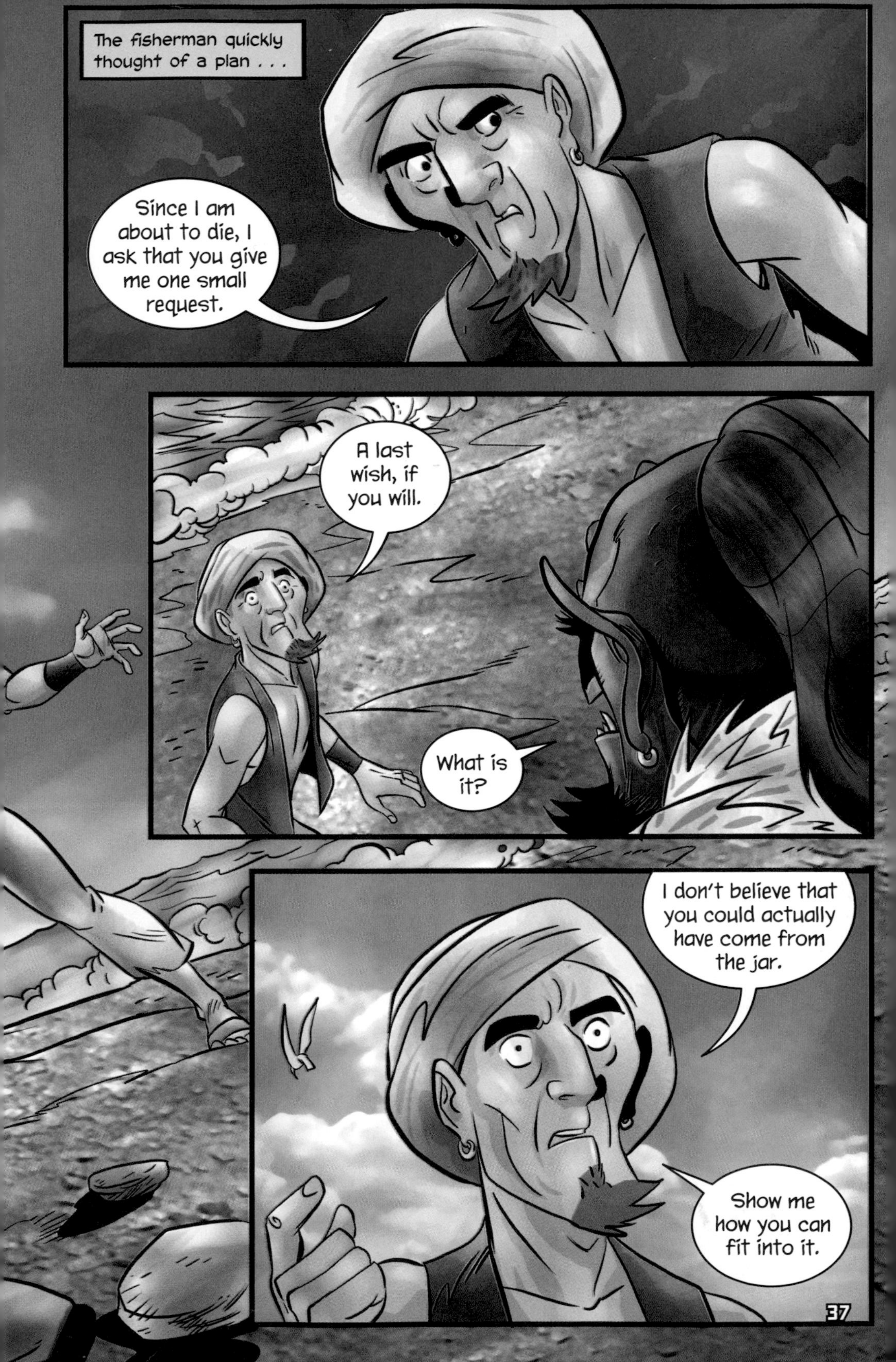
The fisherman quickly thought of a plan . . .
Since I am about to die, I ask that you give me one small request.
A last wish, if you will.
What is it?
I don't believe that you could actually have come from the jar.
Show me how you can fit into it.

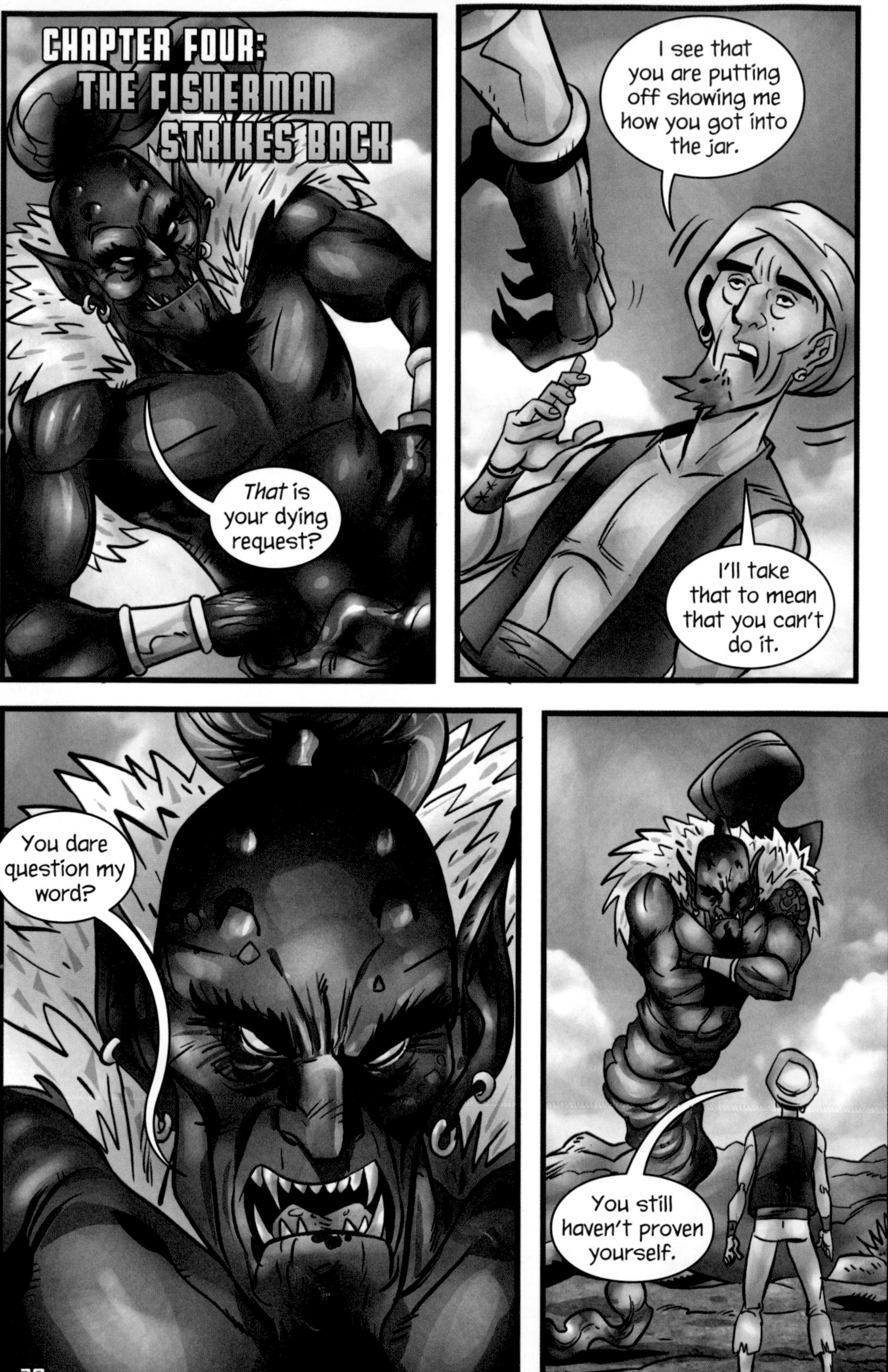
CHAPTER FOUR: THE FISHERMAN STRIKES BACK
That is your dying request?
I see that you are putting off showing me how you got into the jar.
I'll take that to mean that you can't do it.
You dare question my word?
You still haven't proven yourself.

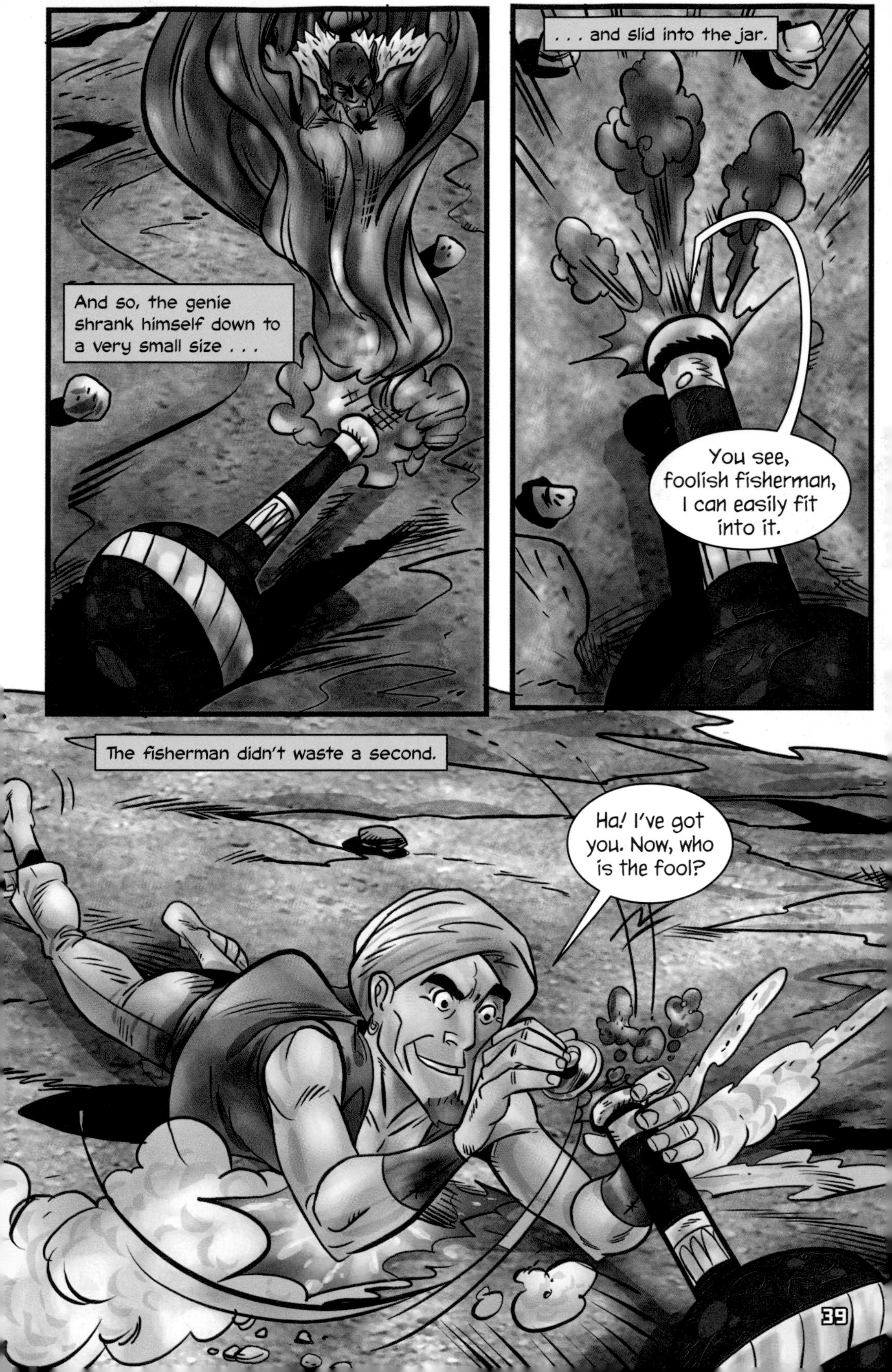
And so, the genie shrank himself down to a very small size . . .
. . . and slid into the jar.
You see, foolish fisherman, I can easily fit into it.
The fisherman didn't waste a second.
Ha! I've got you. Now, who is the fool?

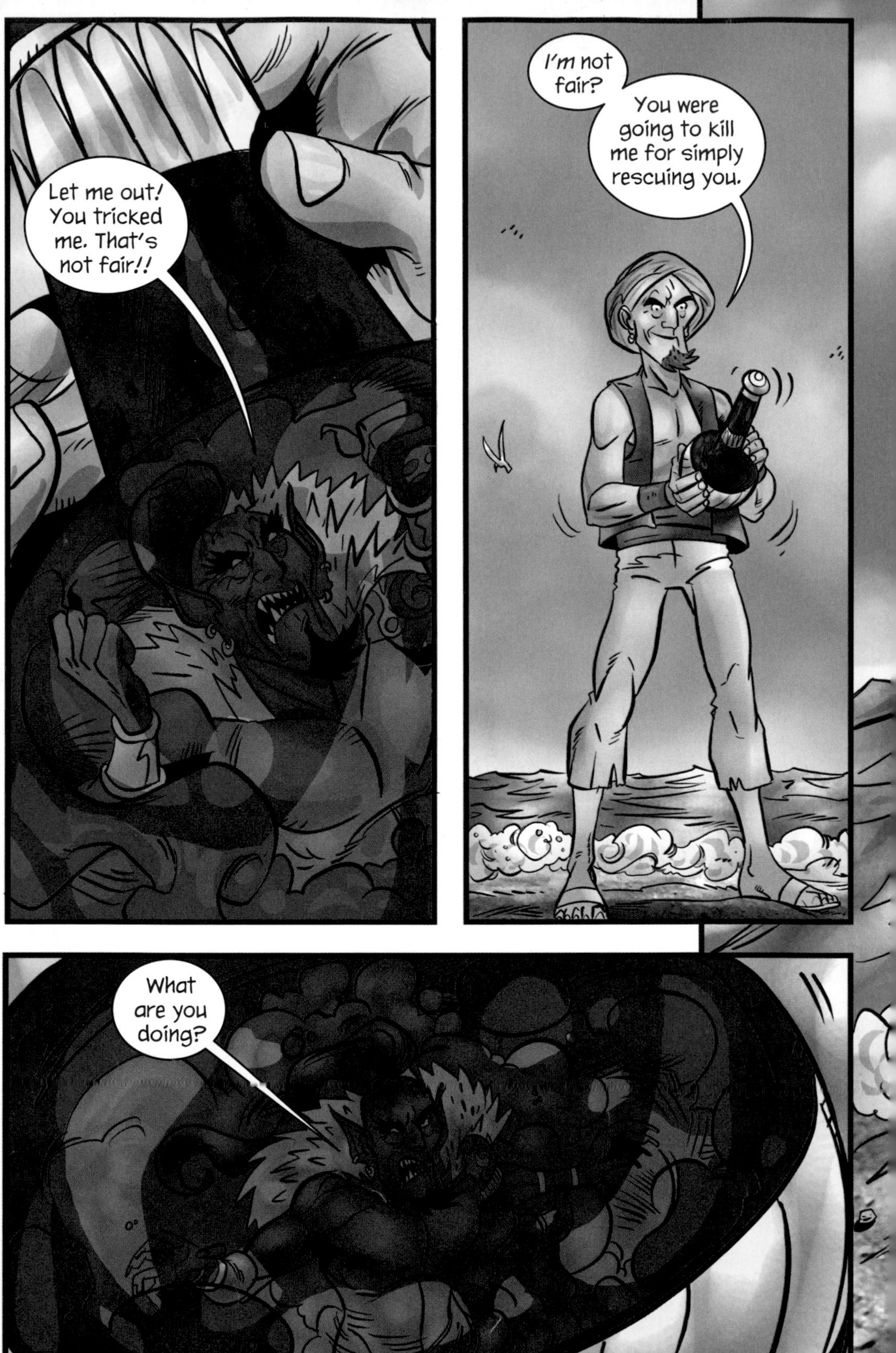
Let me out! You tricked me. That's not fair!!
I'm not fair?
You were going to kill me for simply rescuing you.
What are you doing?

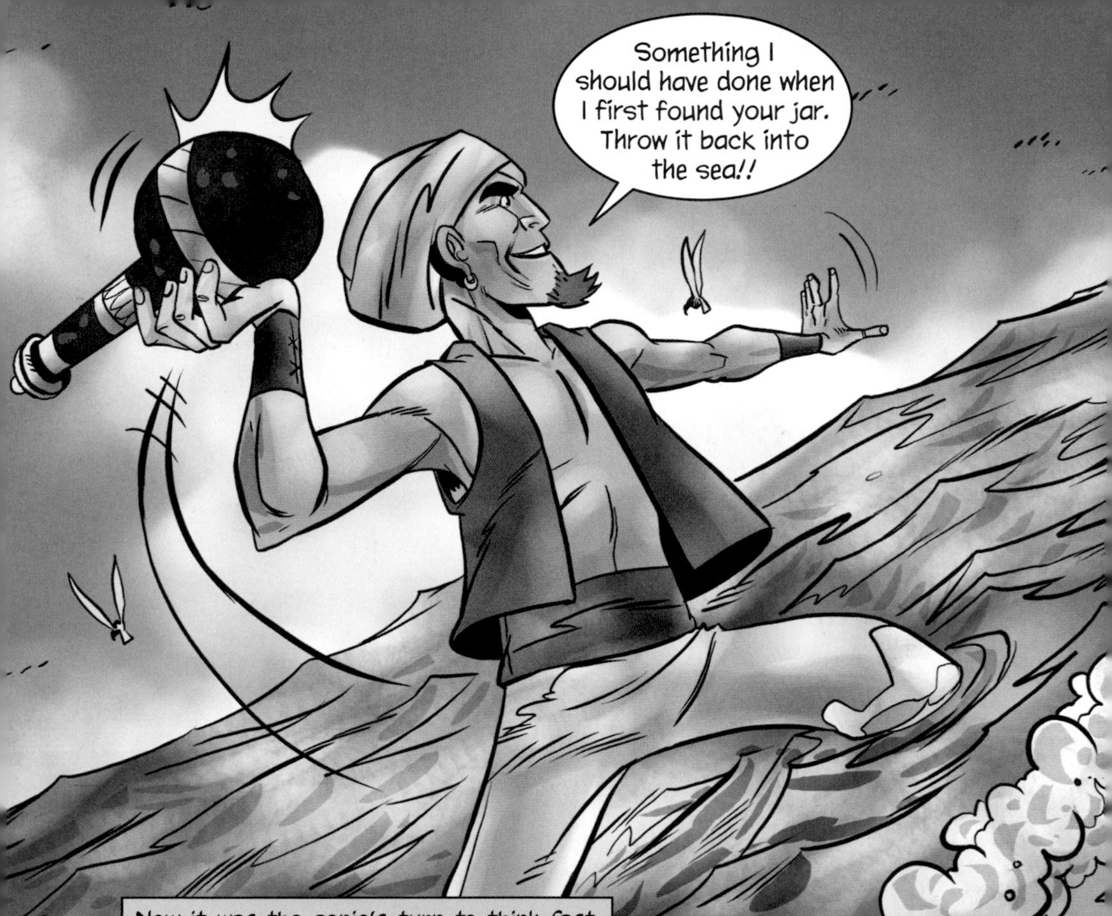
Something I should have done when I first found your jar. Throw it back into the sea!!

Now it was the genie's turn to think fast.

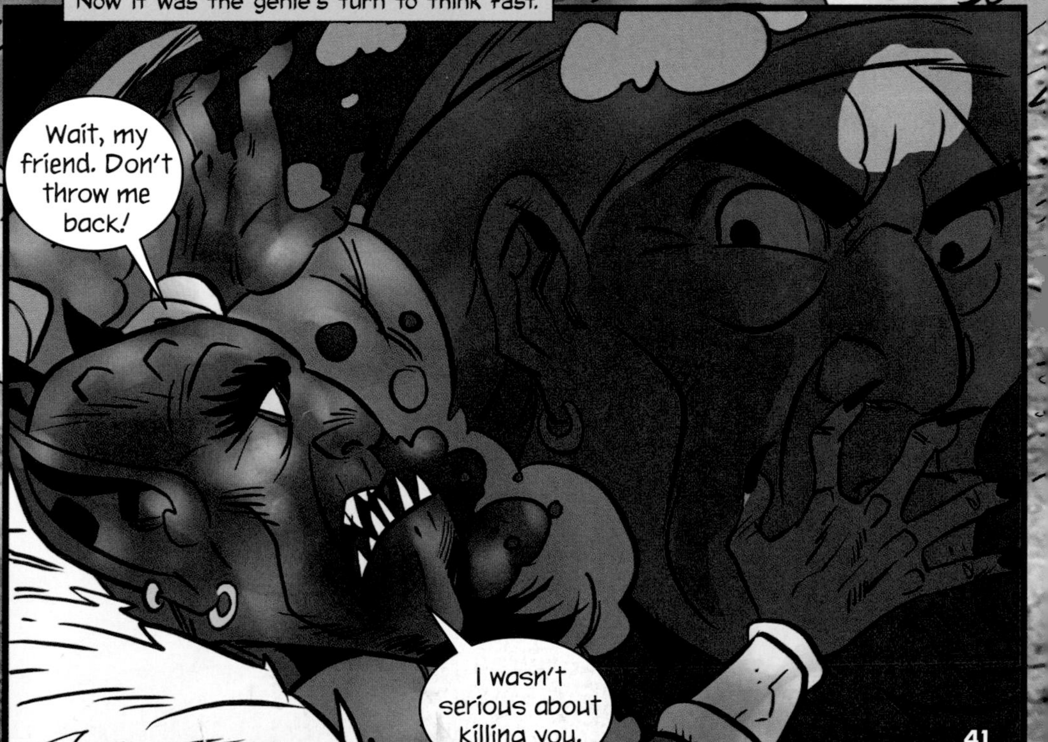
Wait, my friend. Don't throw me back!
I wasn't serious about killing you.

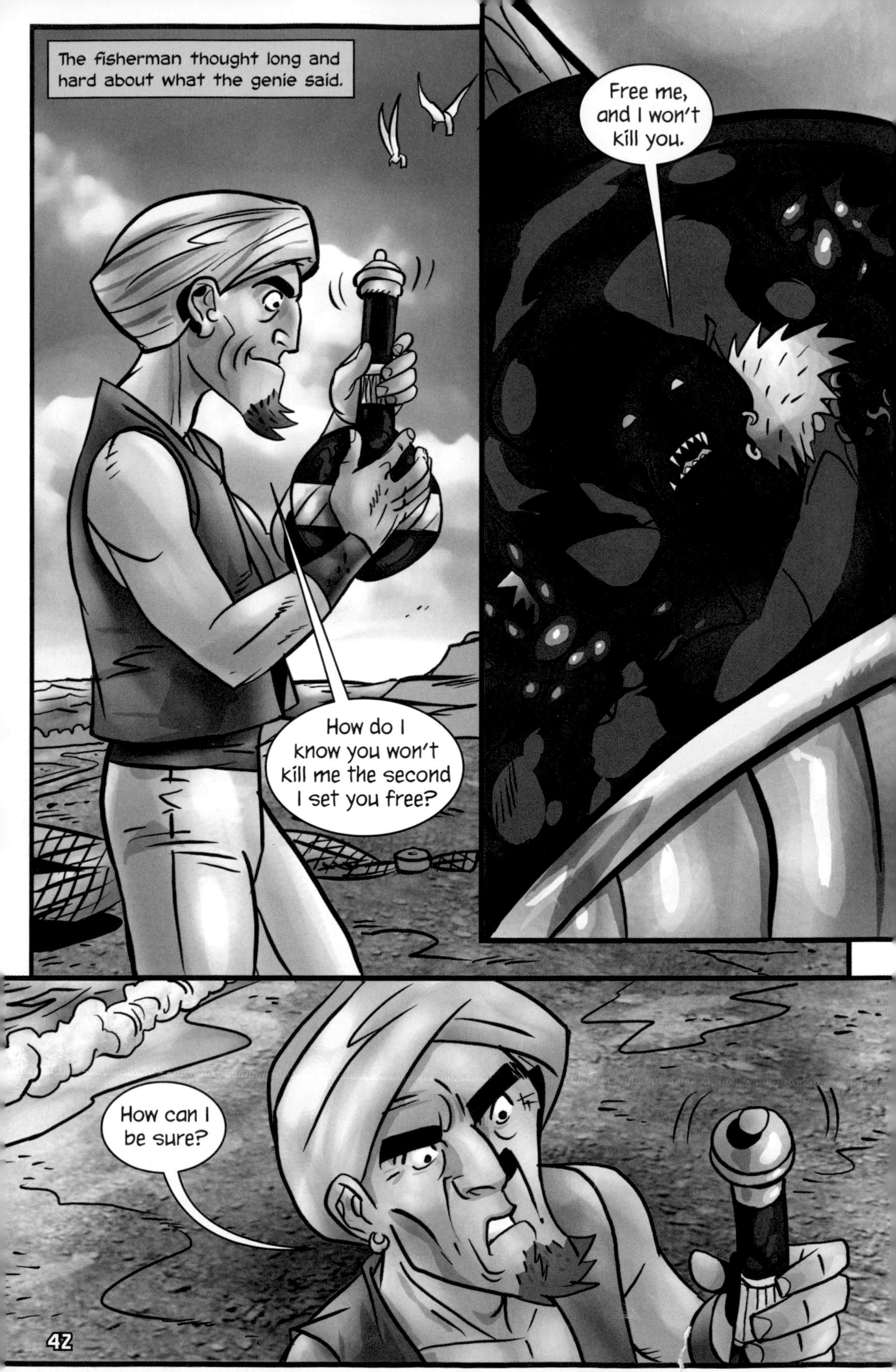

The fisherman thought long and hard about what the genie said.
How do I know you won't kill me the second I set you free?
Free me, and I won't kill you.
How can I be sure?

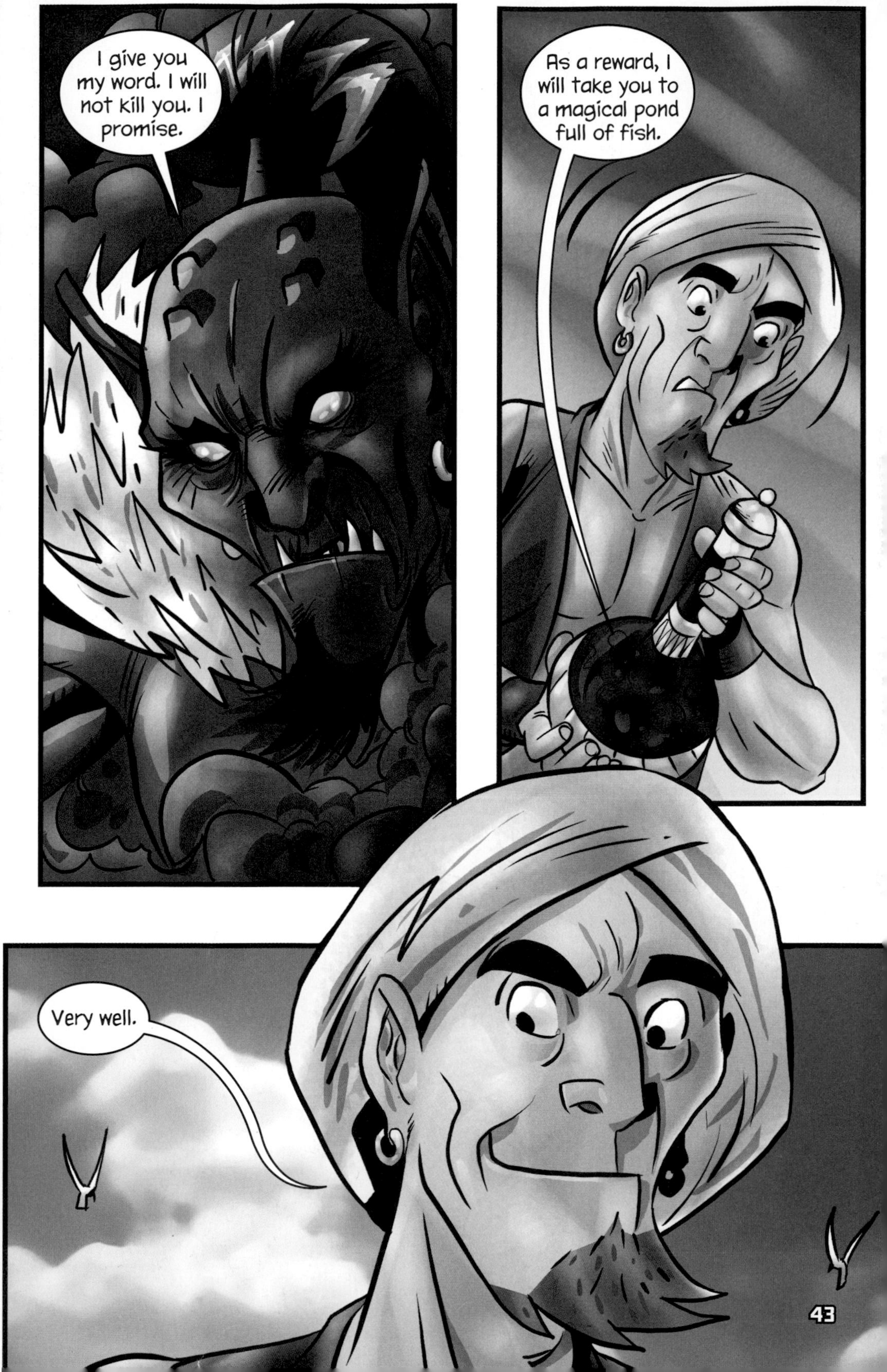
I give you my word. I will not kill you. I promise.
As a reward, I will take you to a magical pond full of fish.
Very well.

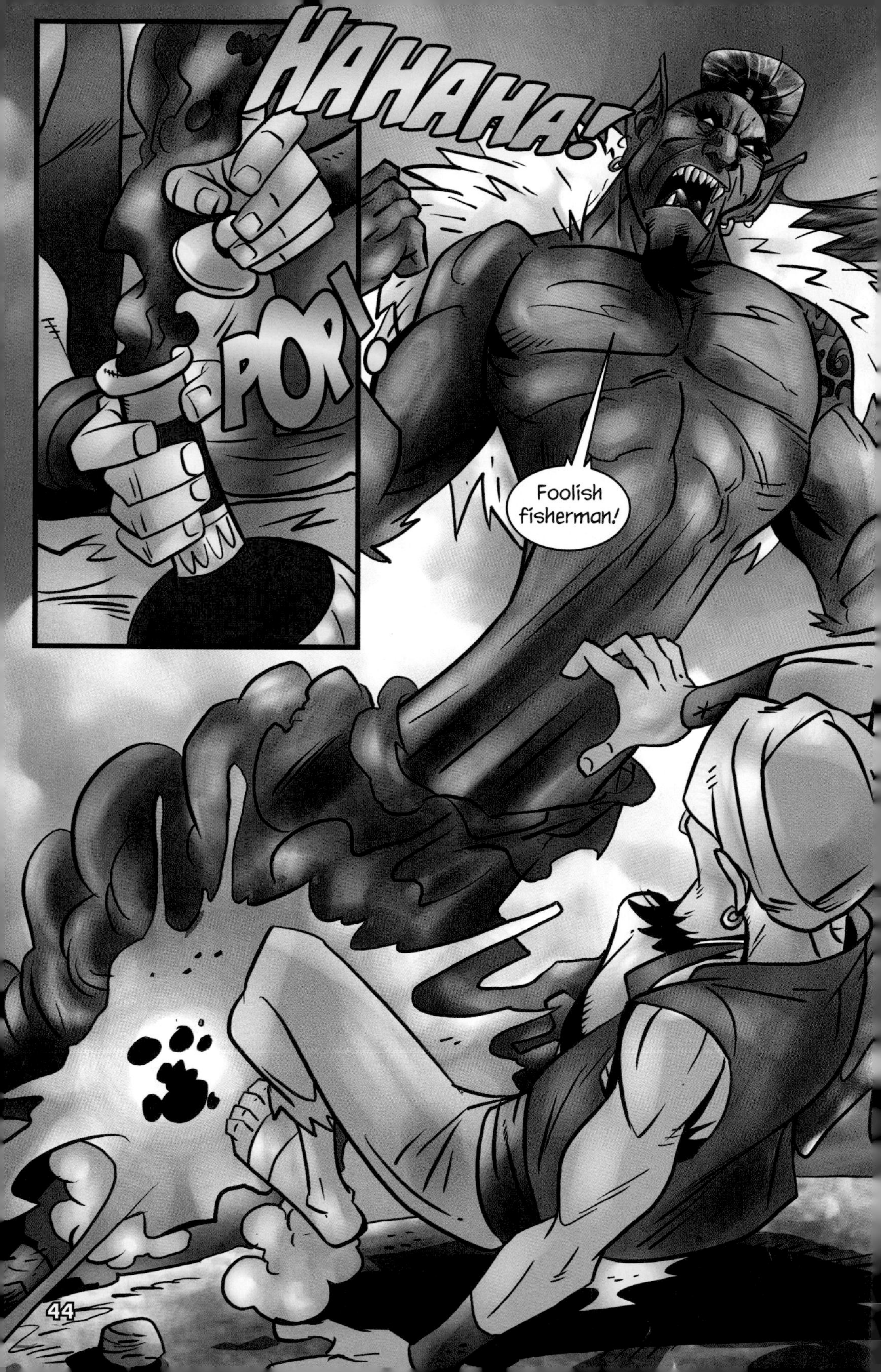

HAHAHA!
POP!
Foolish fisherman!

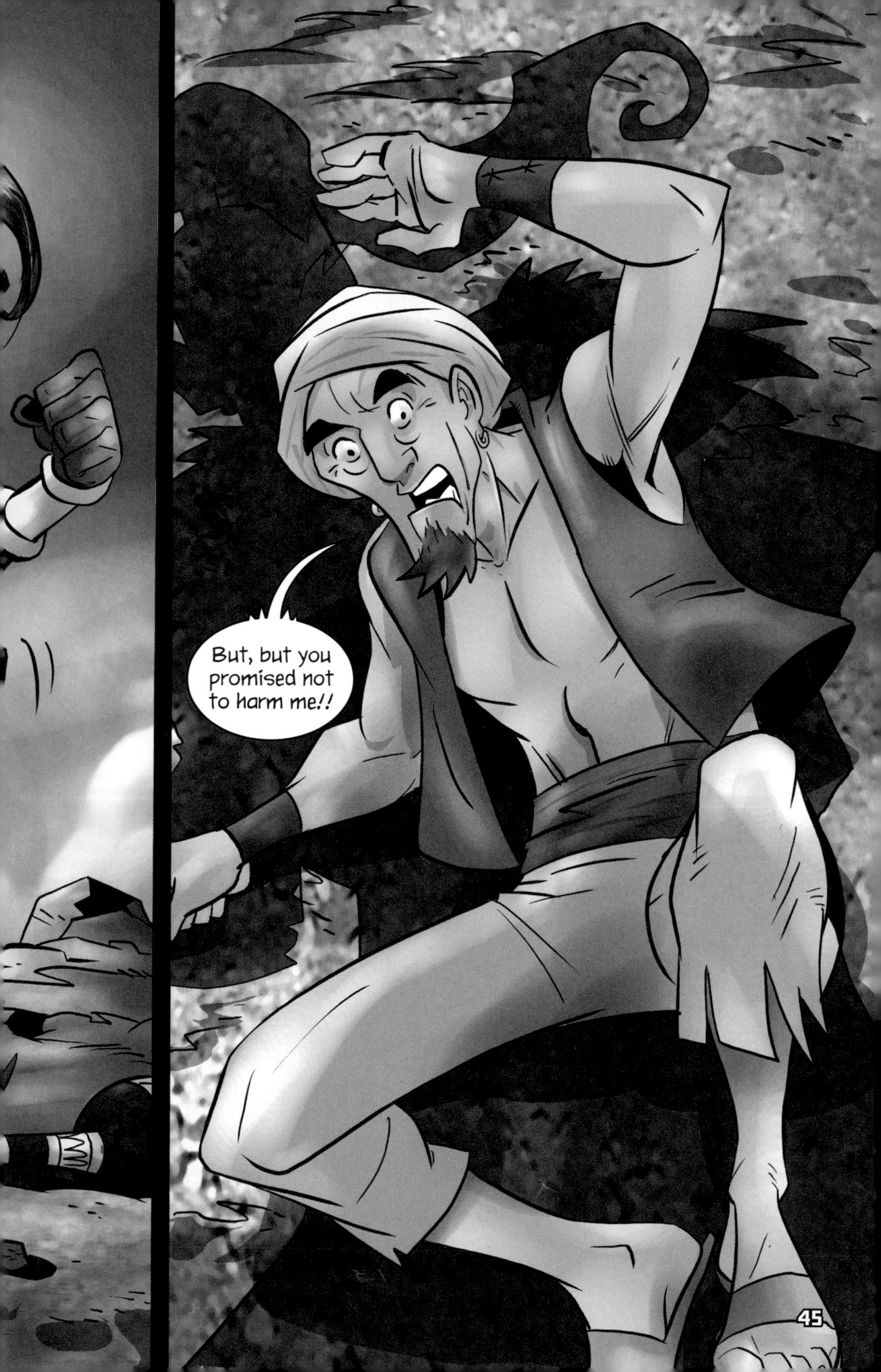
But, but you promised not to harm me!!

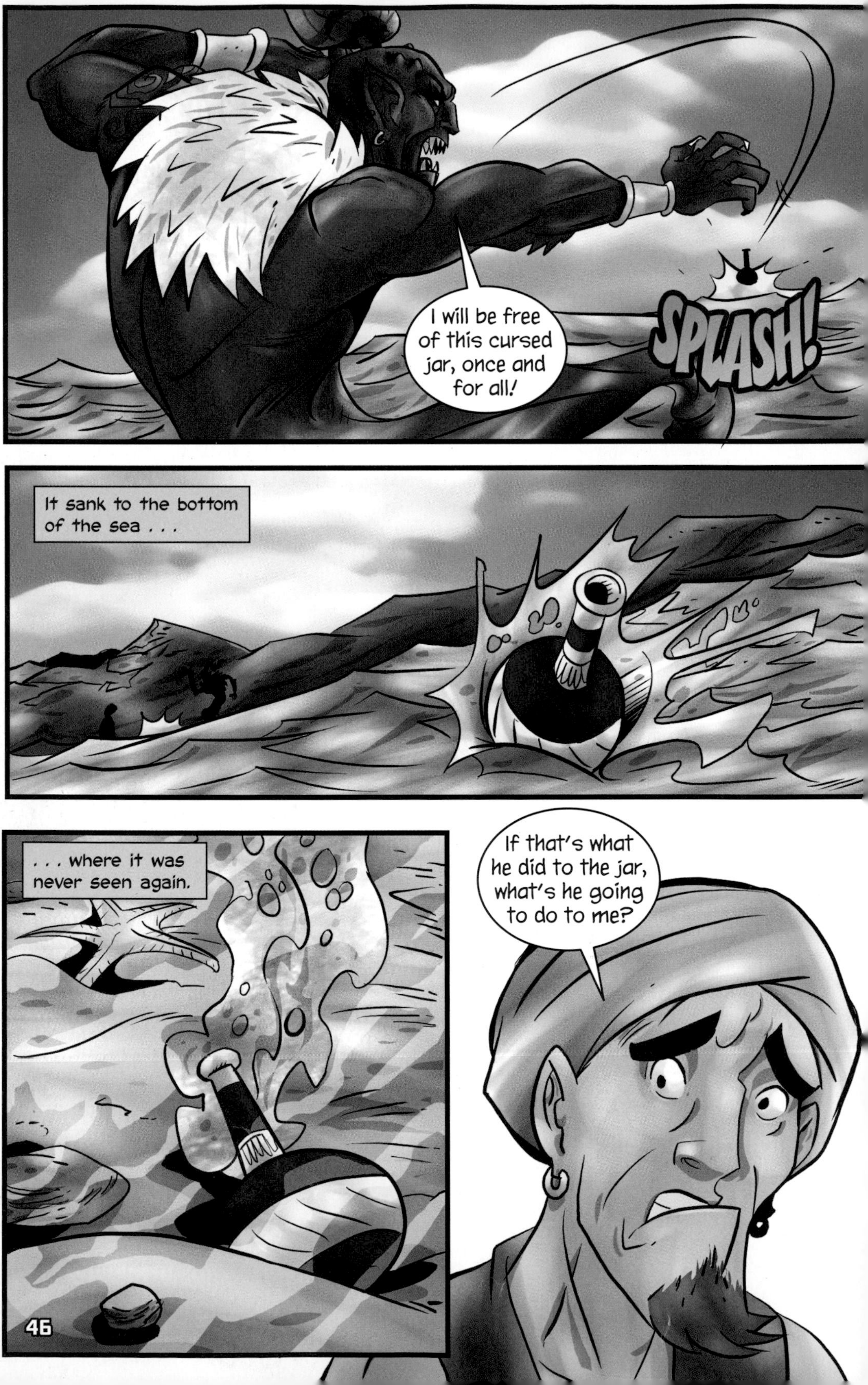
I will be free of this cursed jar, once and for all!
SPLASH!
It sank to the bottom of the sea . . .
. . . where it was never seen again.
If that's what he did to the jar, what's he going to do to me?

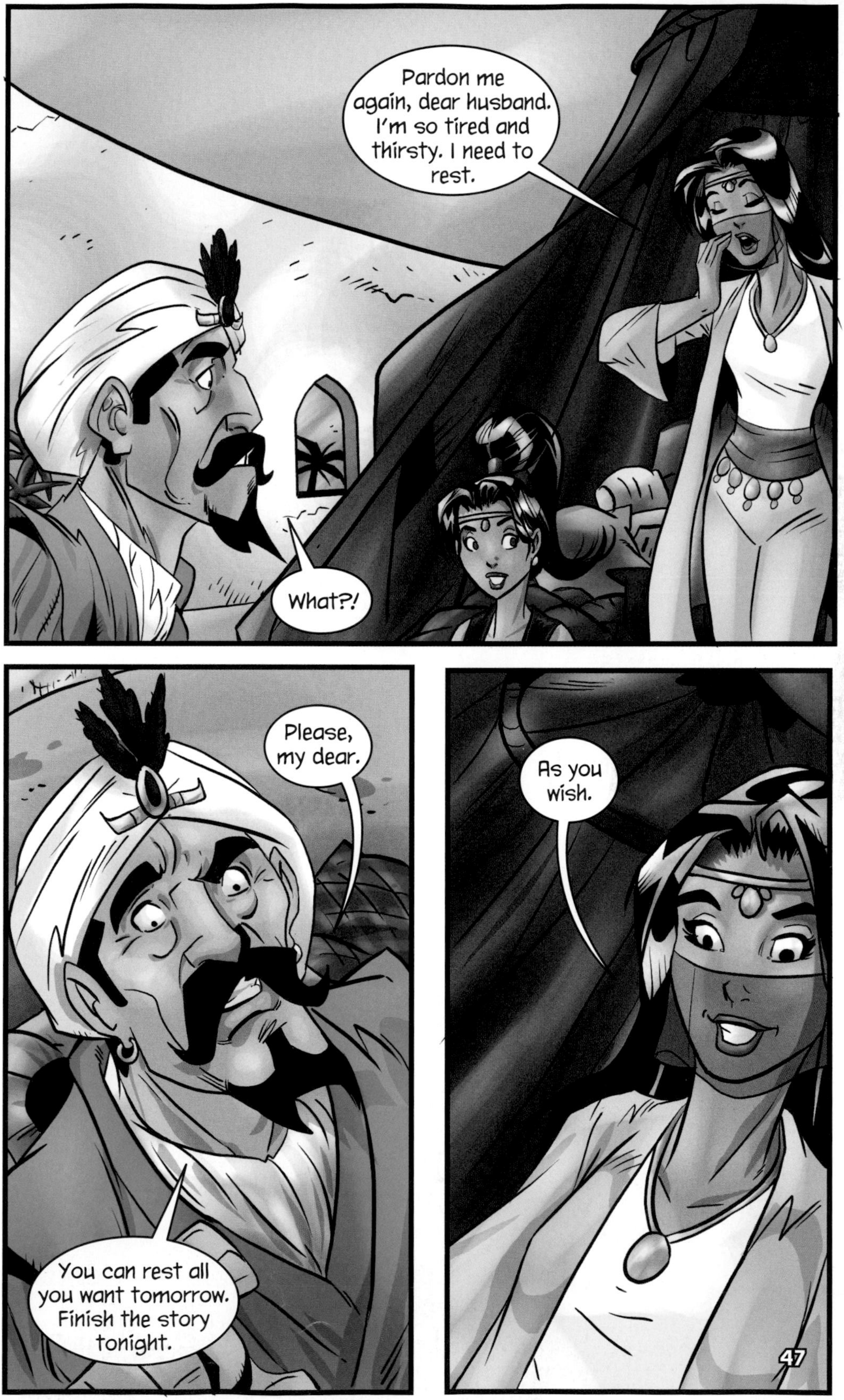
Pardon me again, dear husband. I'm so tired and thirsty. I need to rest.
What?!
Please, my dear.
You can rest all you want tomorrow. Finish the story tonight.
As you wish.

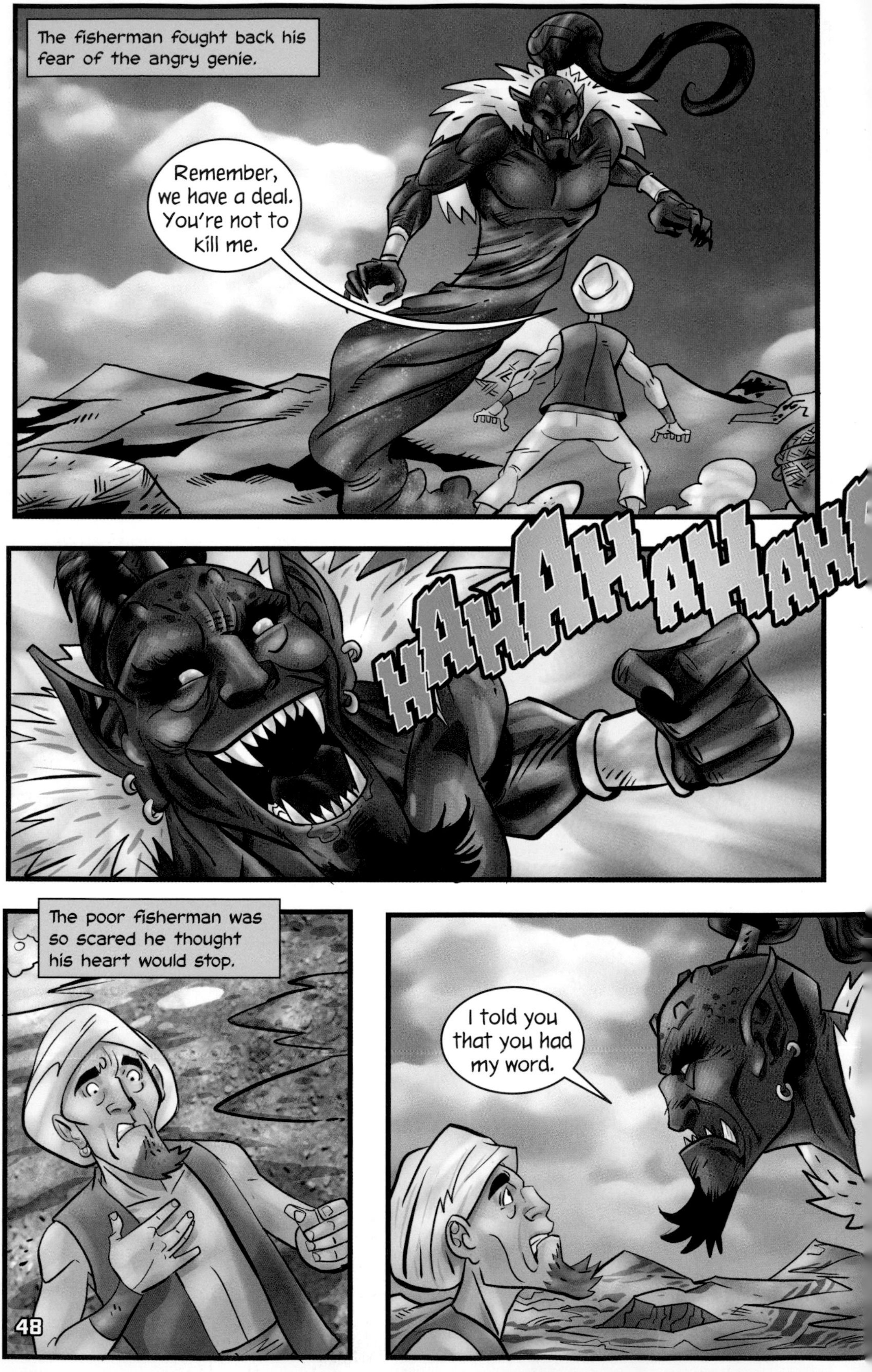

The fisherman fought back his fear of the angry genie.
Remember, we have a deal. You're not to kill me.
HAHAHAHAHAHAH
The poor fisherman was so scared he thought his heart would stop.
I told you that you had my word.

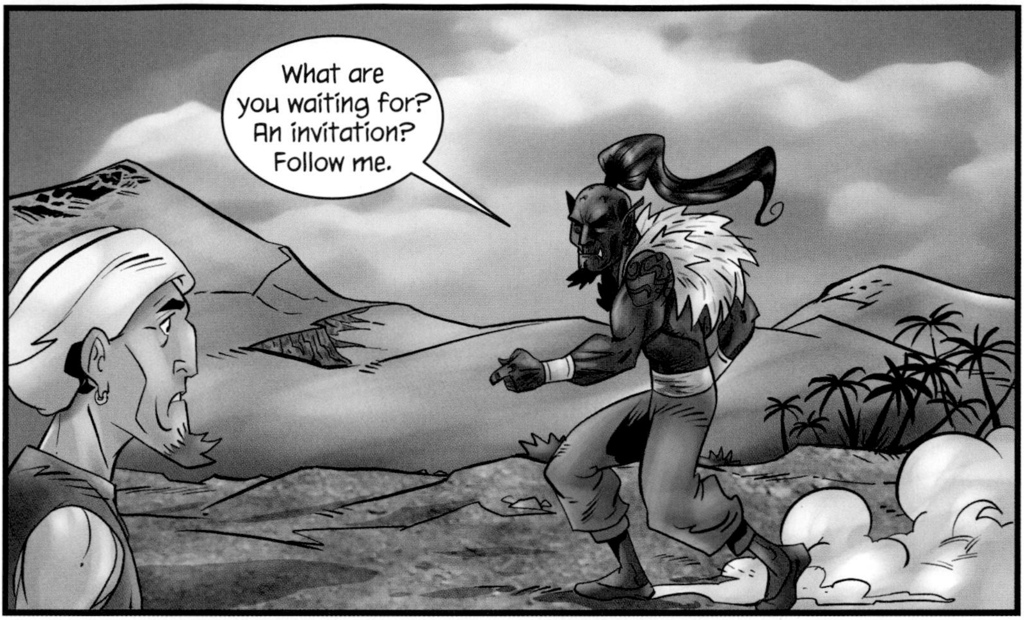
What are you waiting for? An invitation? Follow me.

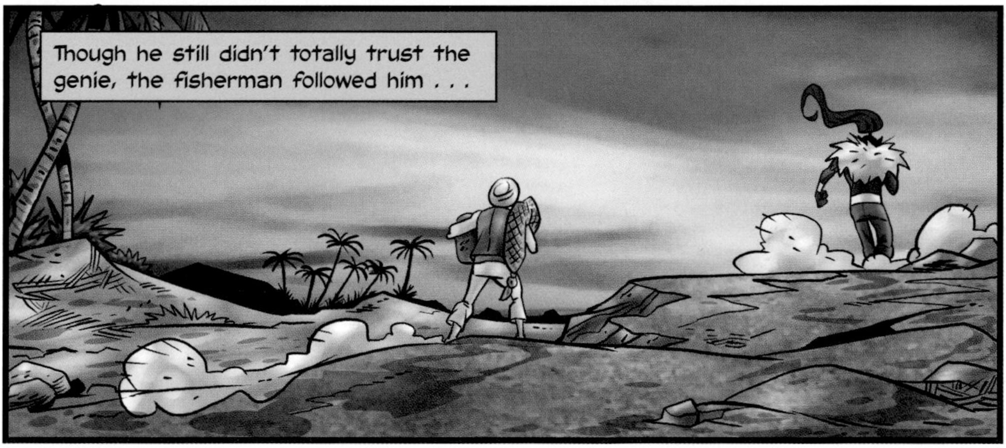
Though he still didn't totally trust the genie, the fisherman followed him . . .

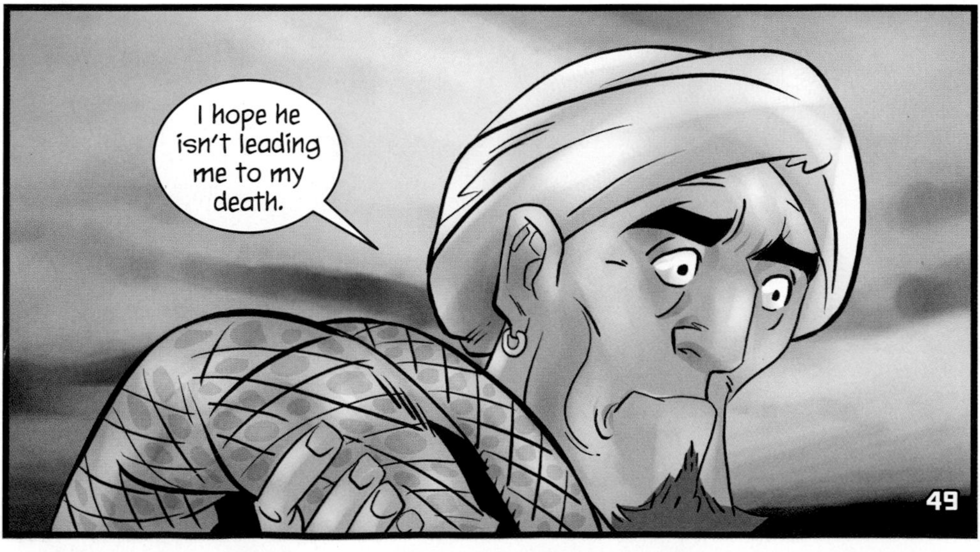
I hope he isn't leading me to my death.
49

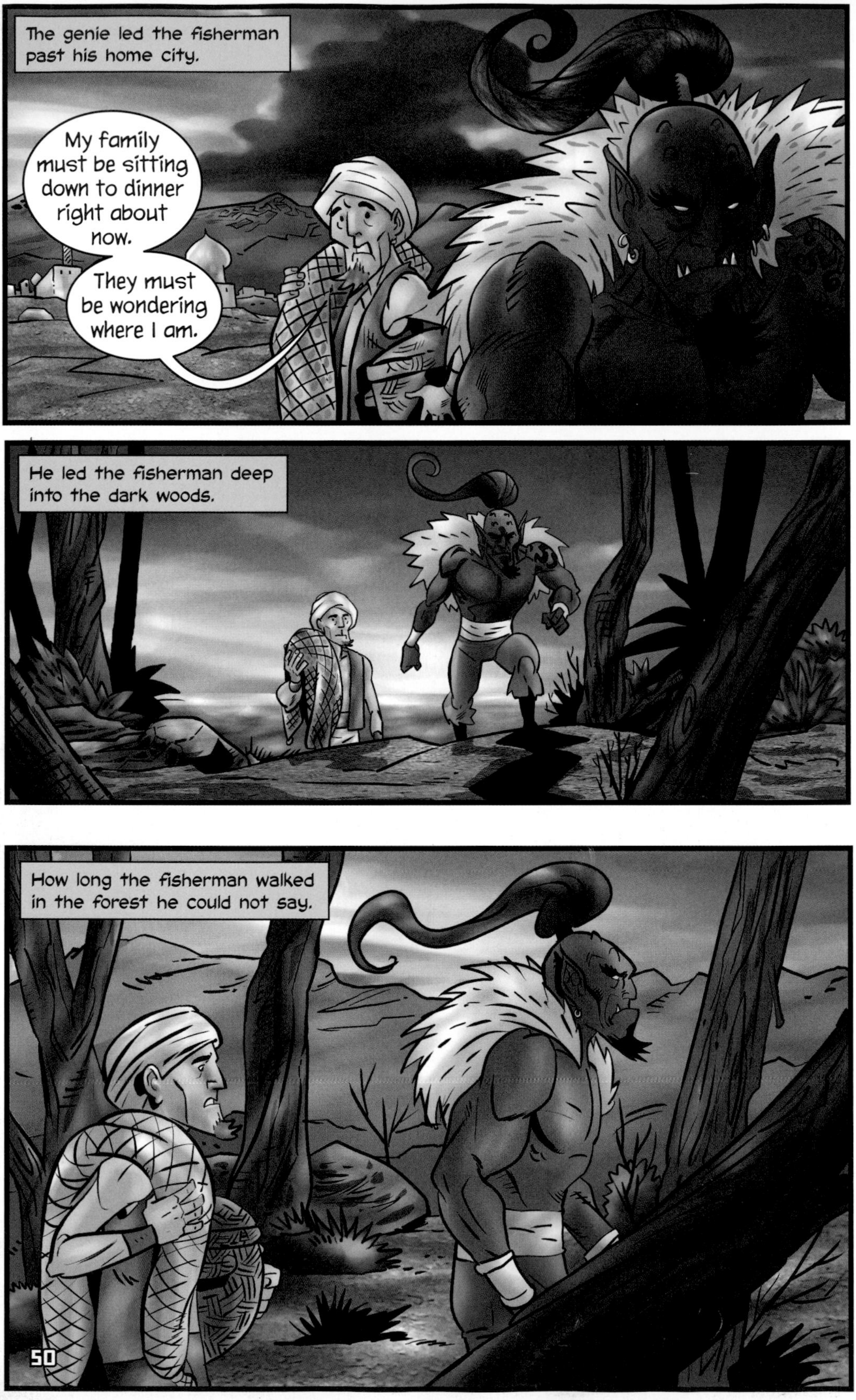
The genie led the fisherman past his home city.
My family must be sitting down to dinner right about now.
They must be wondering where I am.
He led the fisherman deep into the dark woods.
How long the fisherman walked in the forest he could not say.

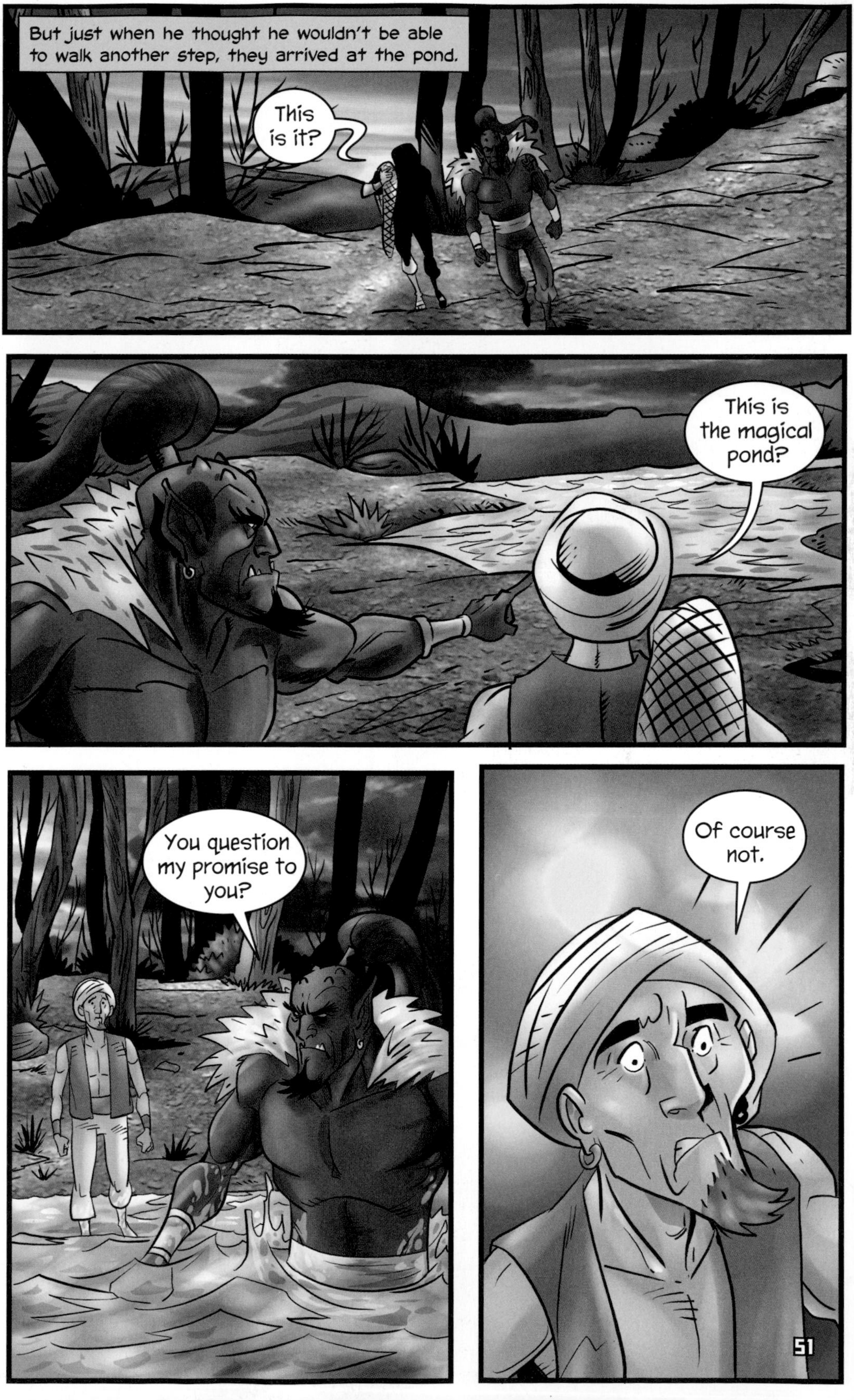

But just when he thought he wouldn't be able to walk another step, they arrived at the pond.
This is it?
This is the magical pond?
You question my promise to you?
Of course not.

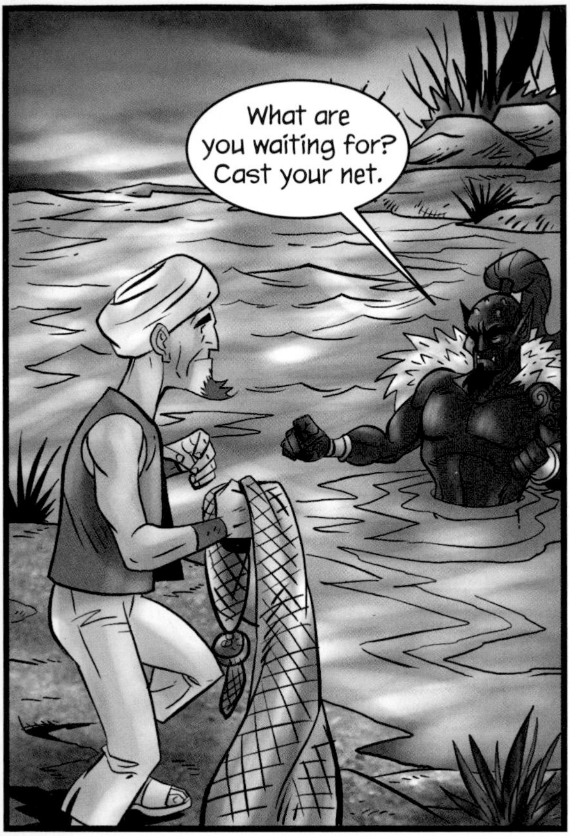
What are you waiting for? Cast your net.

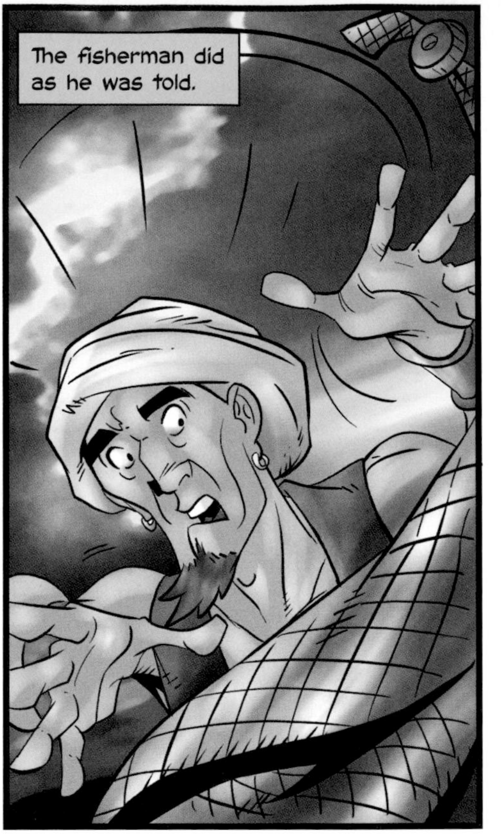
The fisherman did as he was told.

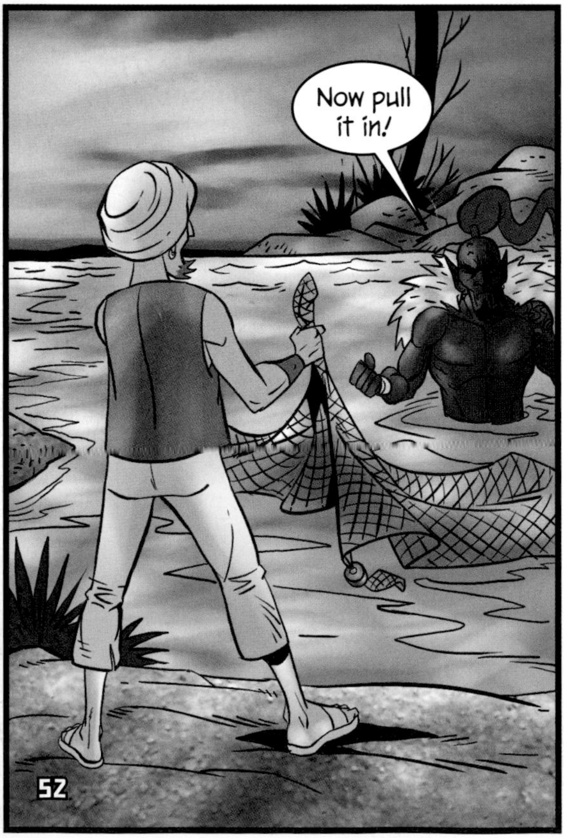
Now pull it in!

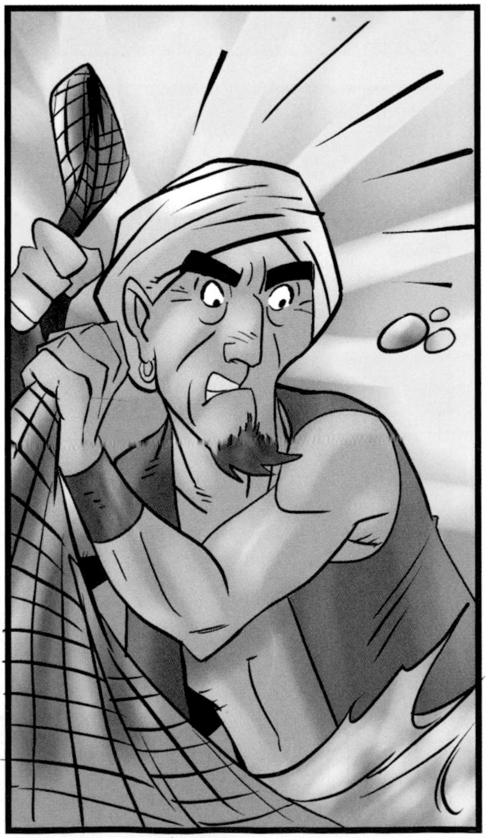

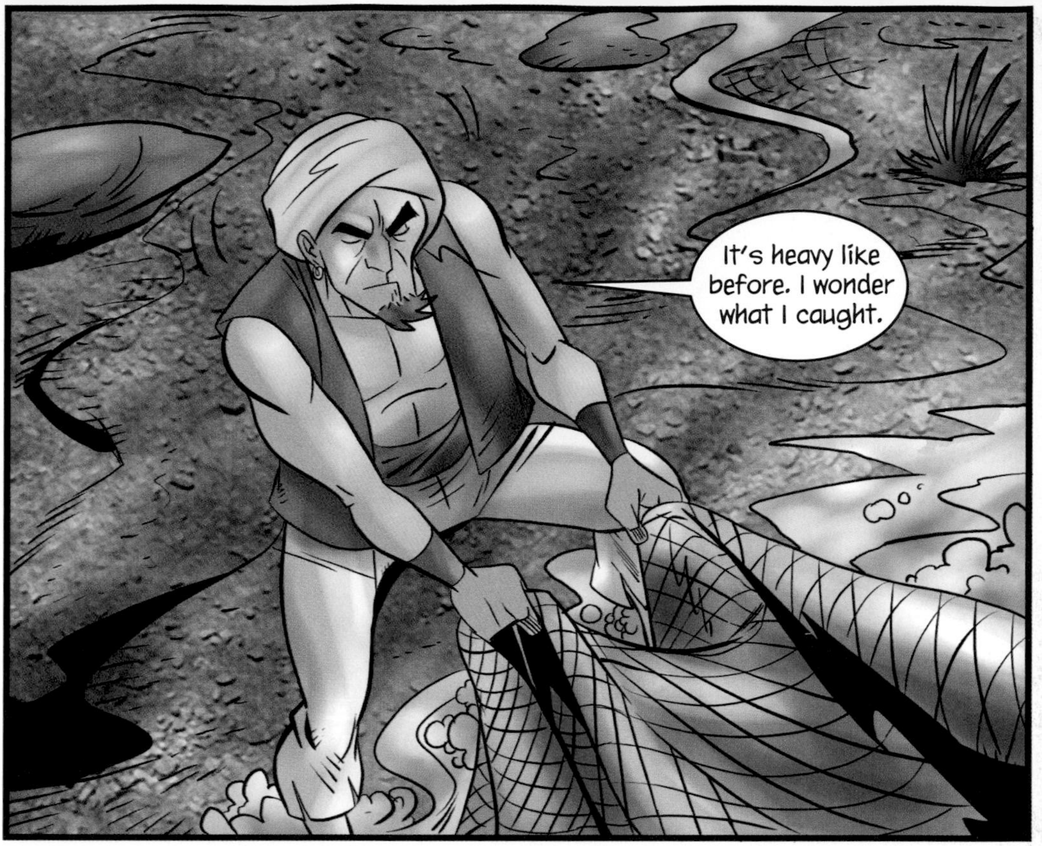
It's heavy like before. I wonder what I caught.

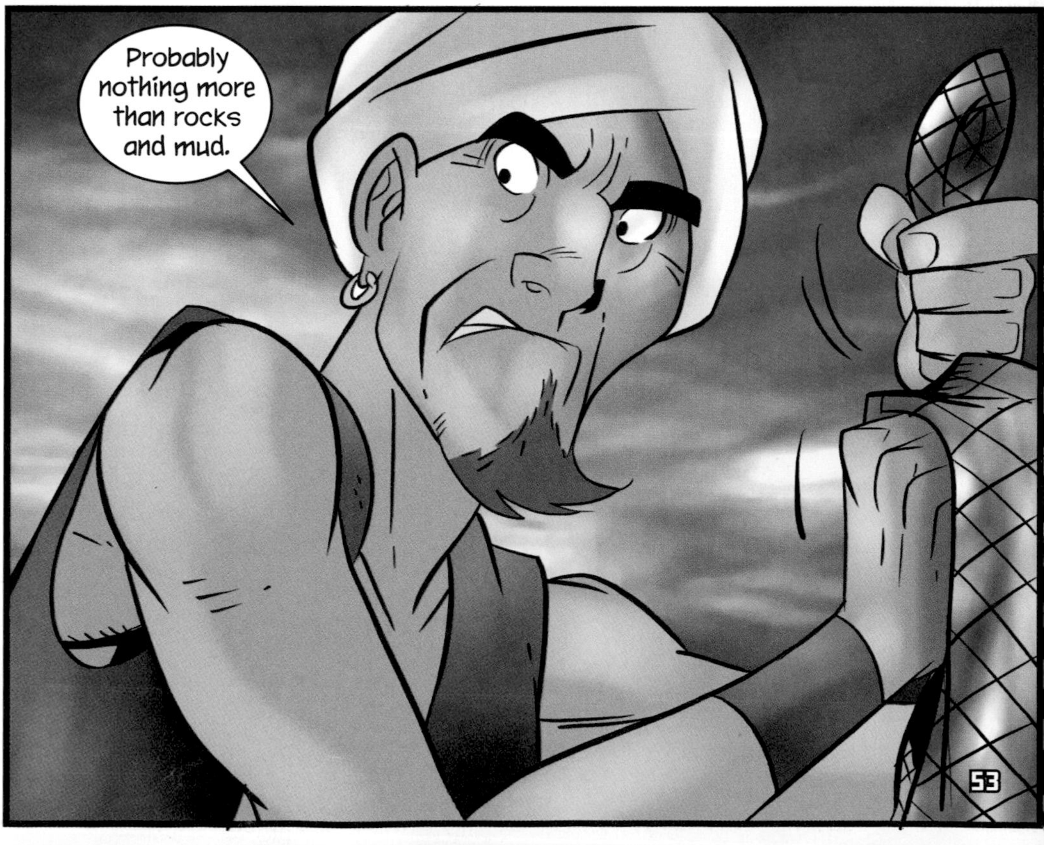
Probably nothing more than rocks and mud.

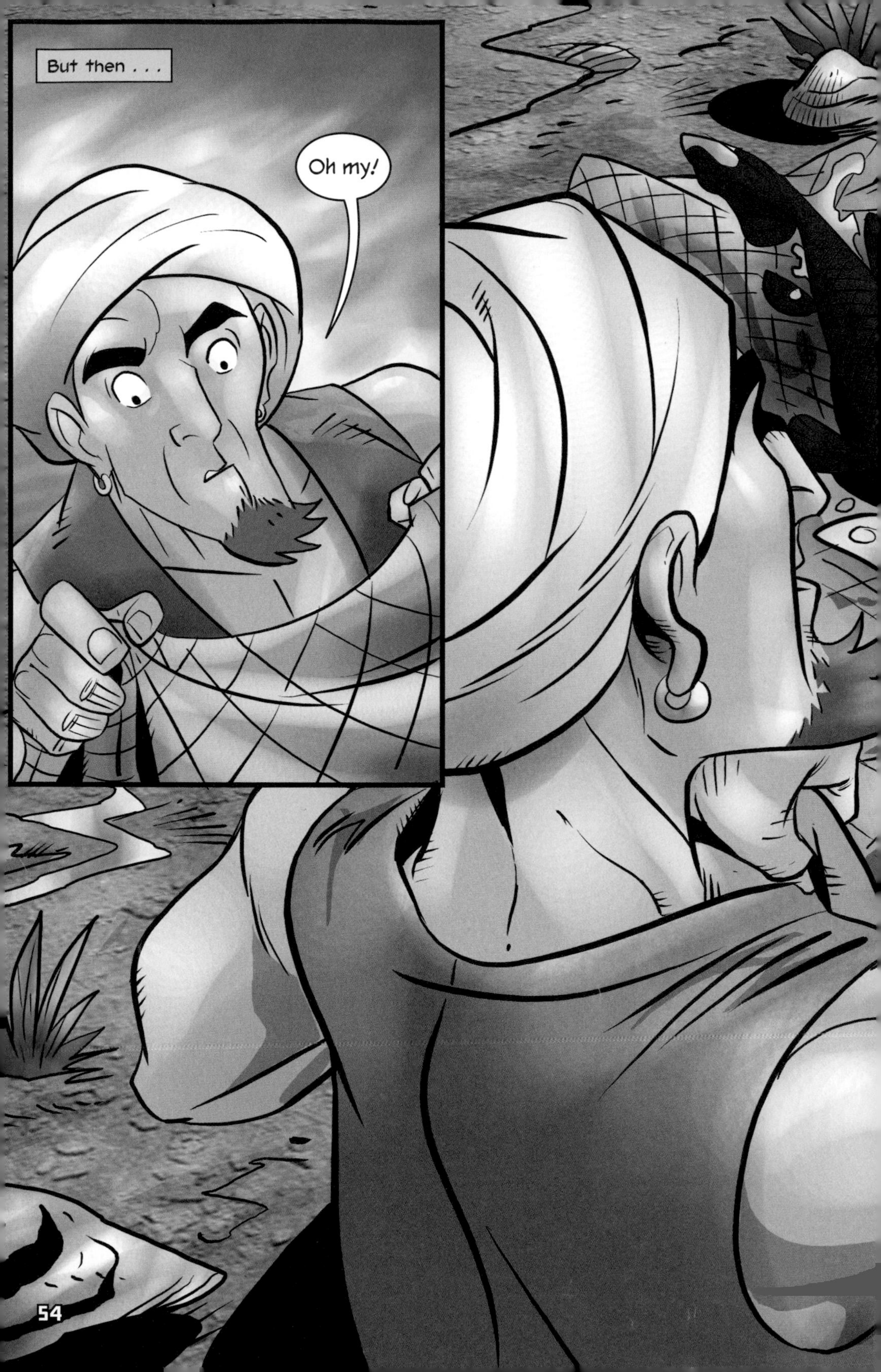
But then . . .
Oh my!

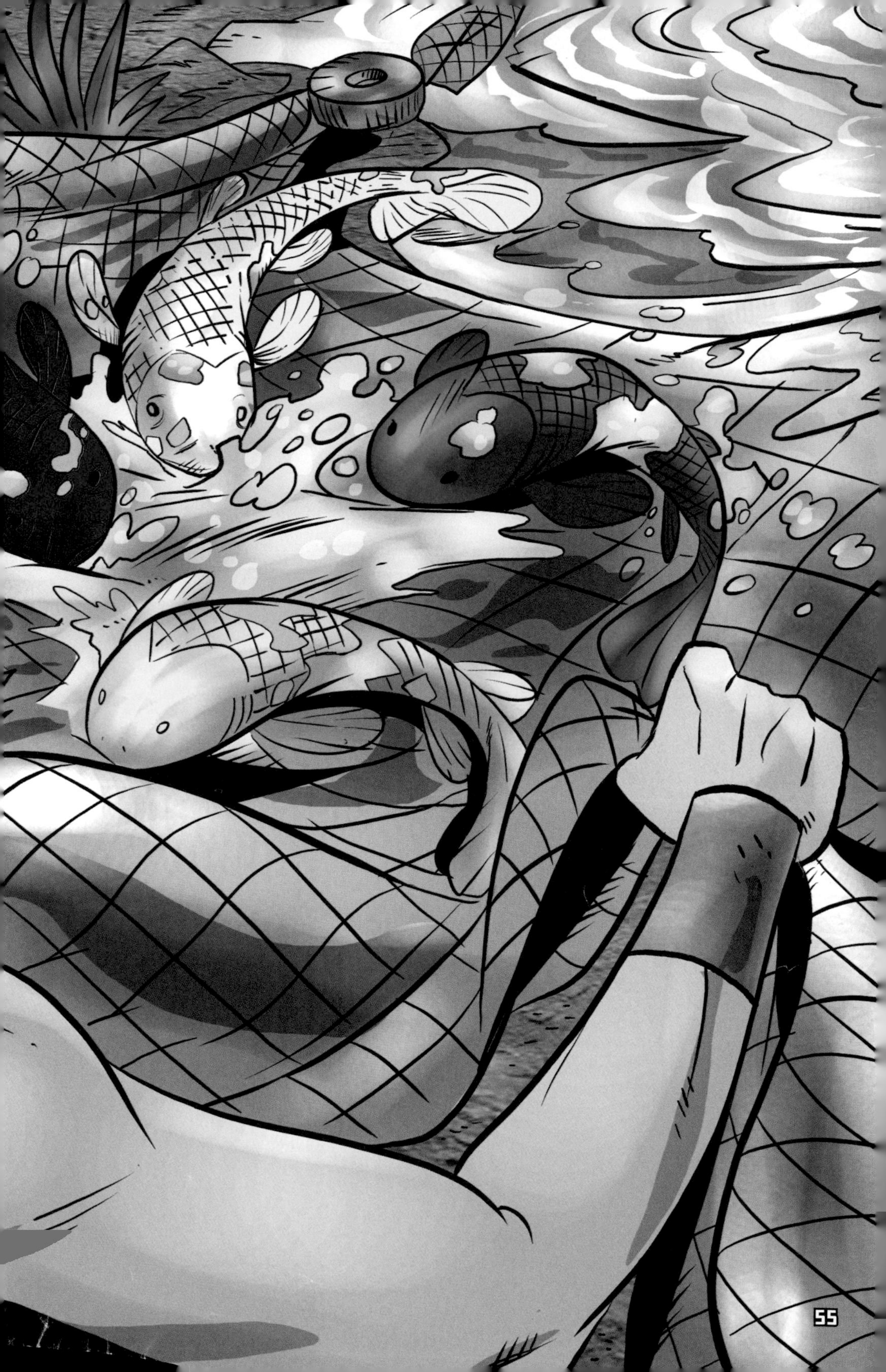

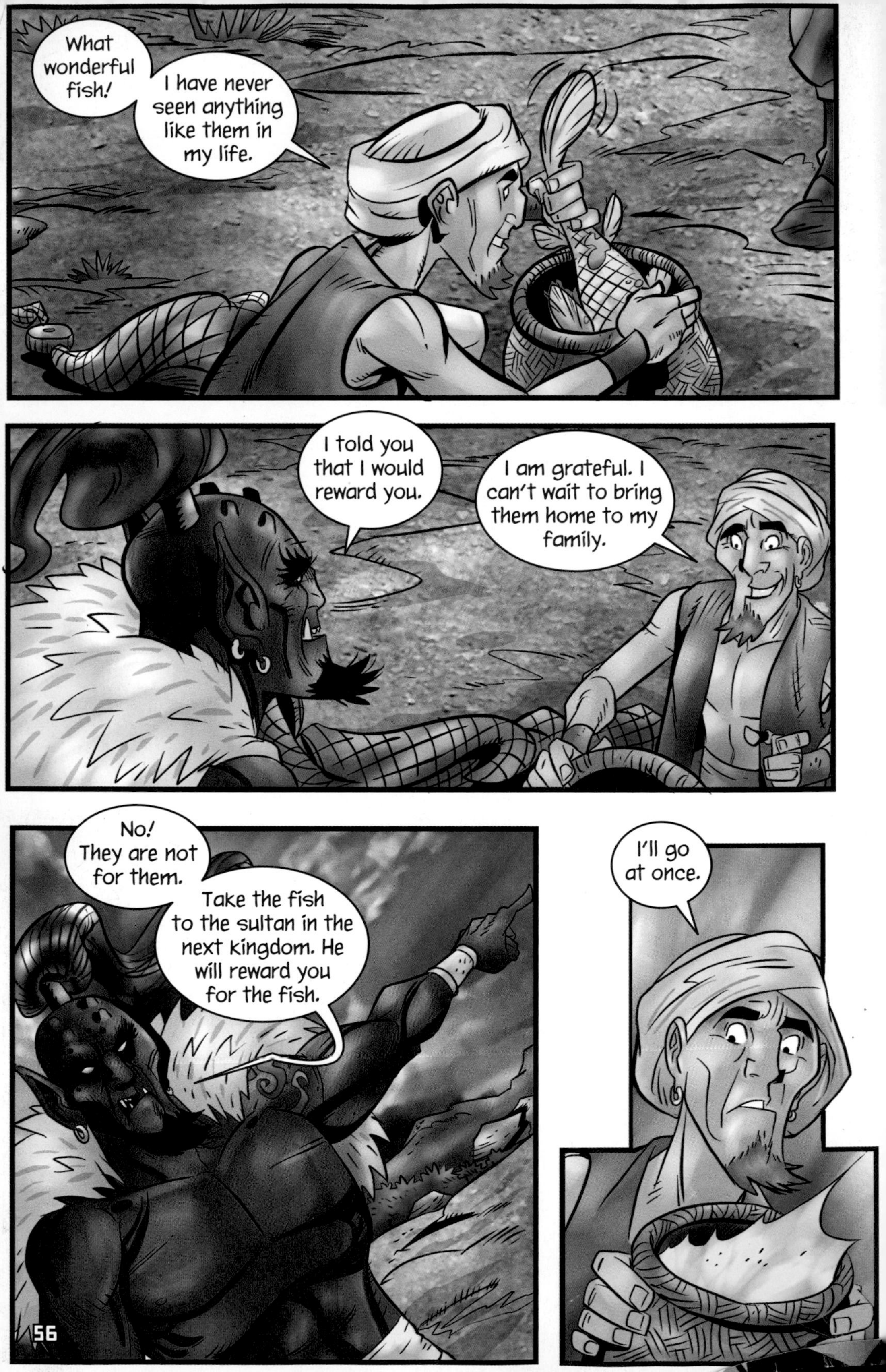
What wonderful fish!
I have never seen anything like them in my life.
I told you that I would reward you.
I am grateful. I can't wait to bring them home to my family.
No! They are not for them.
Take the fish to the sultan in the next kingdom. He will reward you for the fish.
I'll go at once.

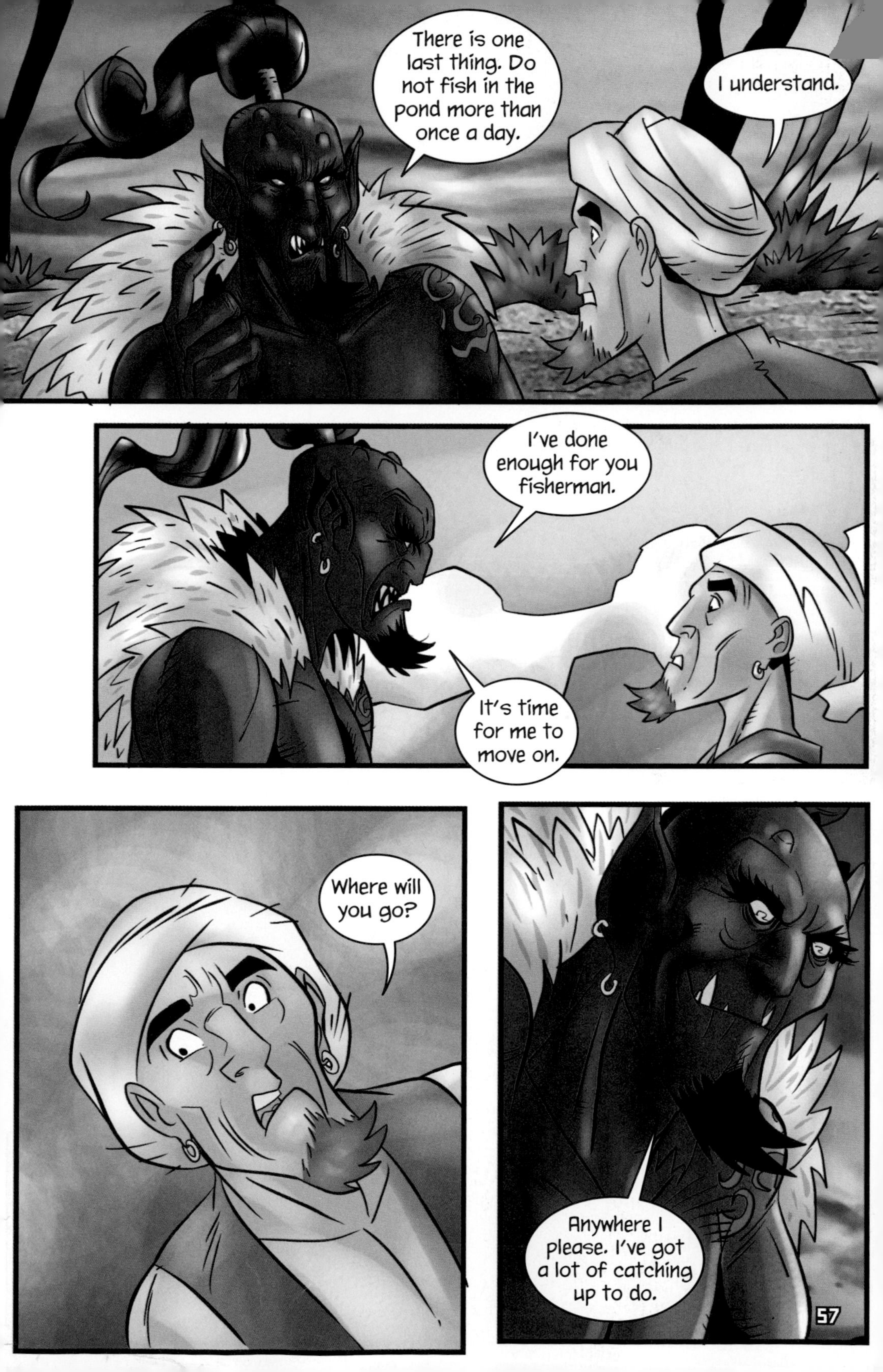
There is one last thing. Do not fish in the pond more than once a day.
I understand.
I've done enough for you fisherman.
It's time for me to move on.
Where will you go?
Anywhere I please. I've got a lot of catching up to do.
57

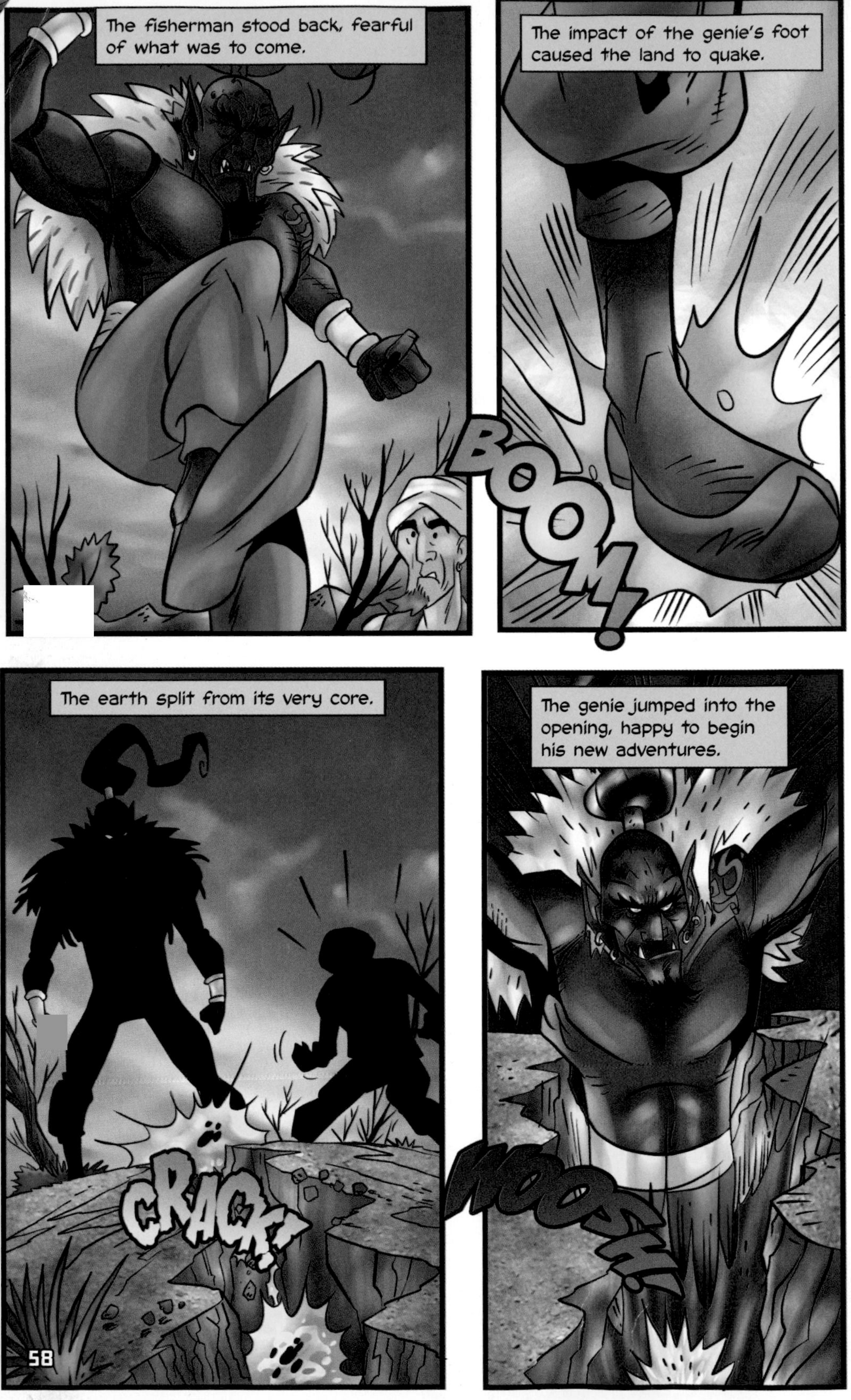
The fisherman stood back, fearful of what was to come.
The impact of the genie's foot caused the land to quake.
BOOM!
The earth split from its very core.
CRACK!
The genie jumped into the opening, happy to begin his new adventures.
WHOOSH!

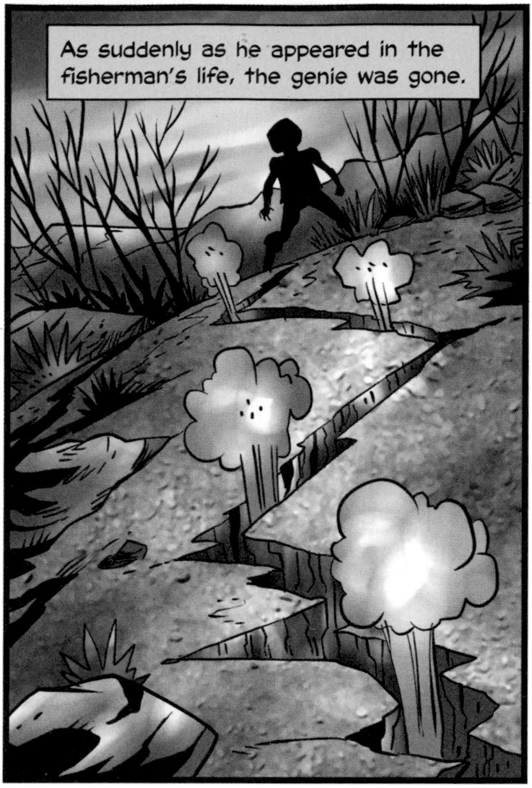
As suddenly as he appeared in the fisherman's life, the genie was gone.

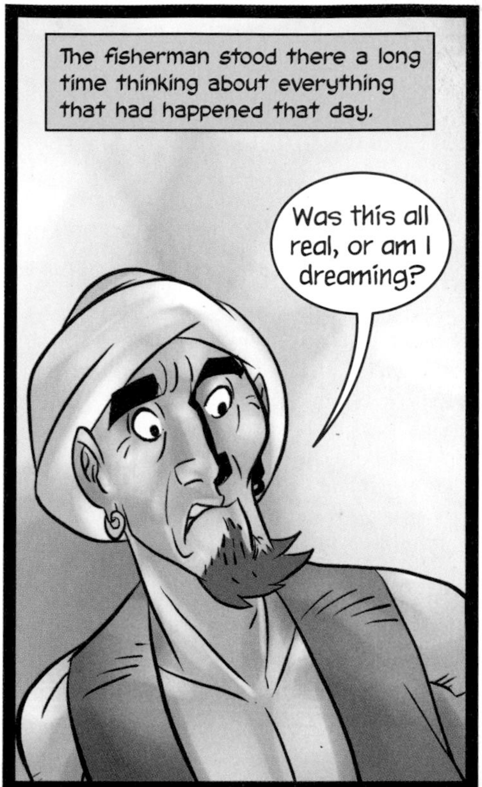
The fisherman stood there a long time thinking about everything that had happened that day.
Was this all real, or am I dreaming?

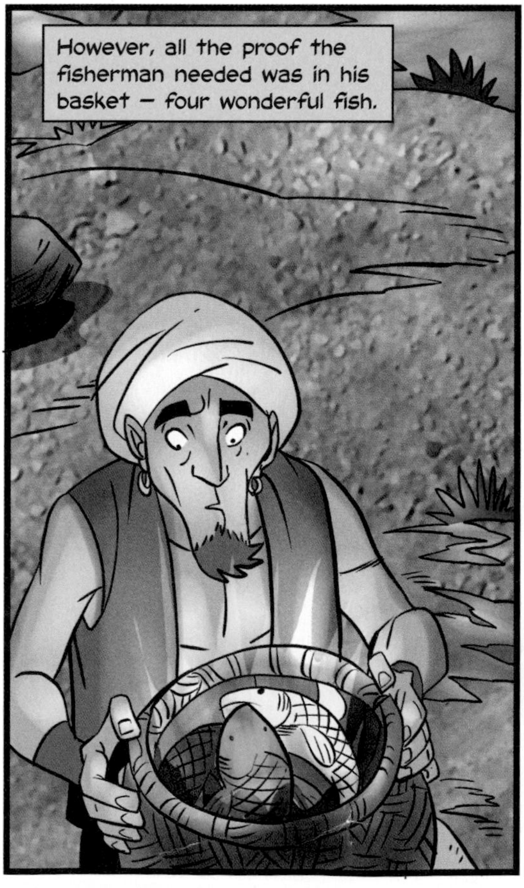
However, all the proof the fisherman needed was in his basket — four wonderful fish.

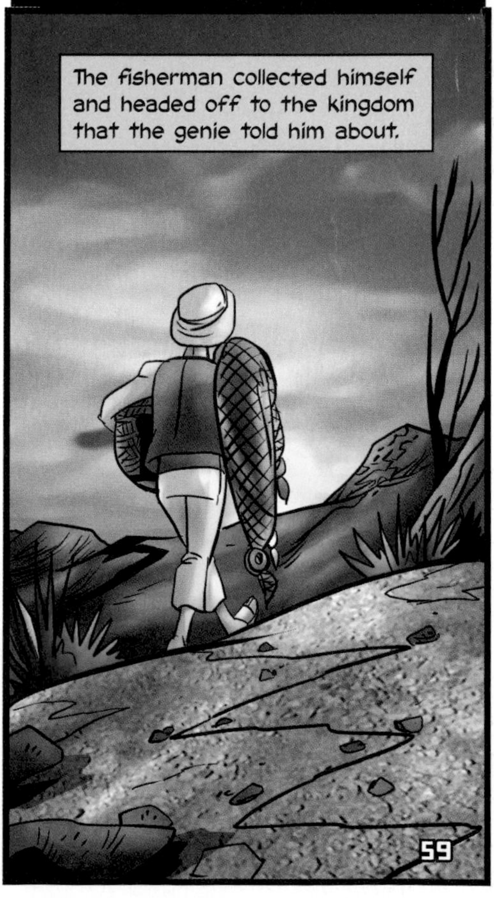
The fisherman collected himself and headed off to the kingdom that the genie told him about.

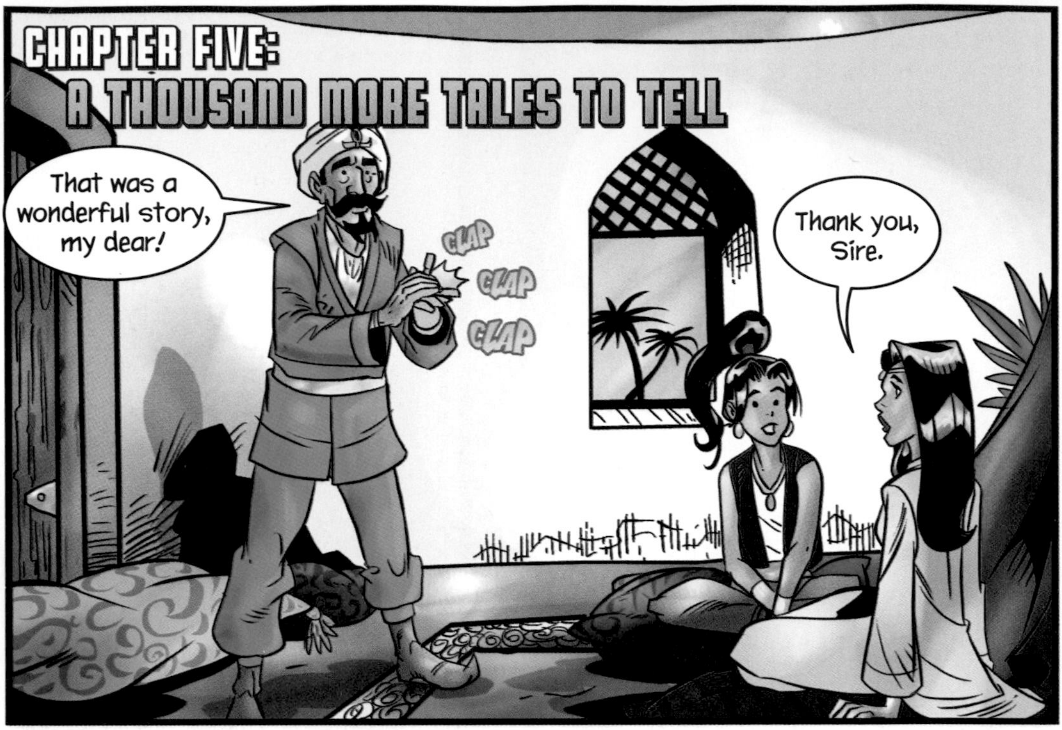
CHAPTER FIVE:
A THOUSAND MORE TALES TO TELL
That was a wonderful story, my dear!
CLAP
CLAP
CLAP
Thank you, Sire.

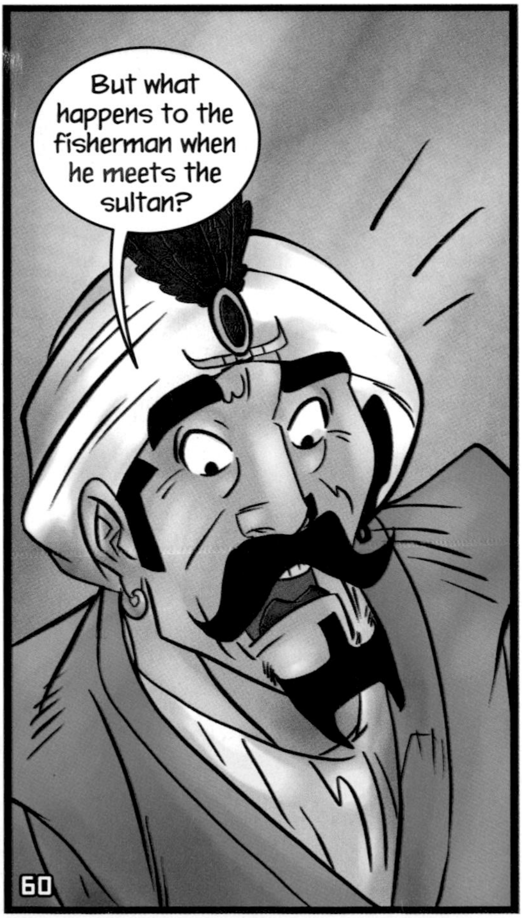
But what happens to the fisherman when he meets the sultan?

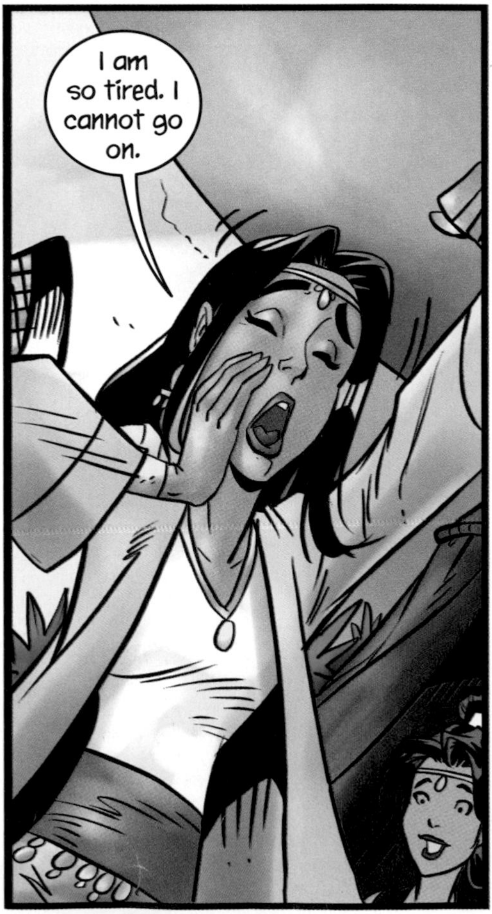
I am so tired. I cannot go on.

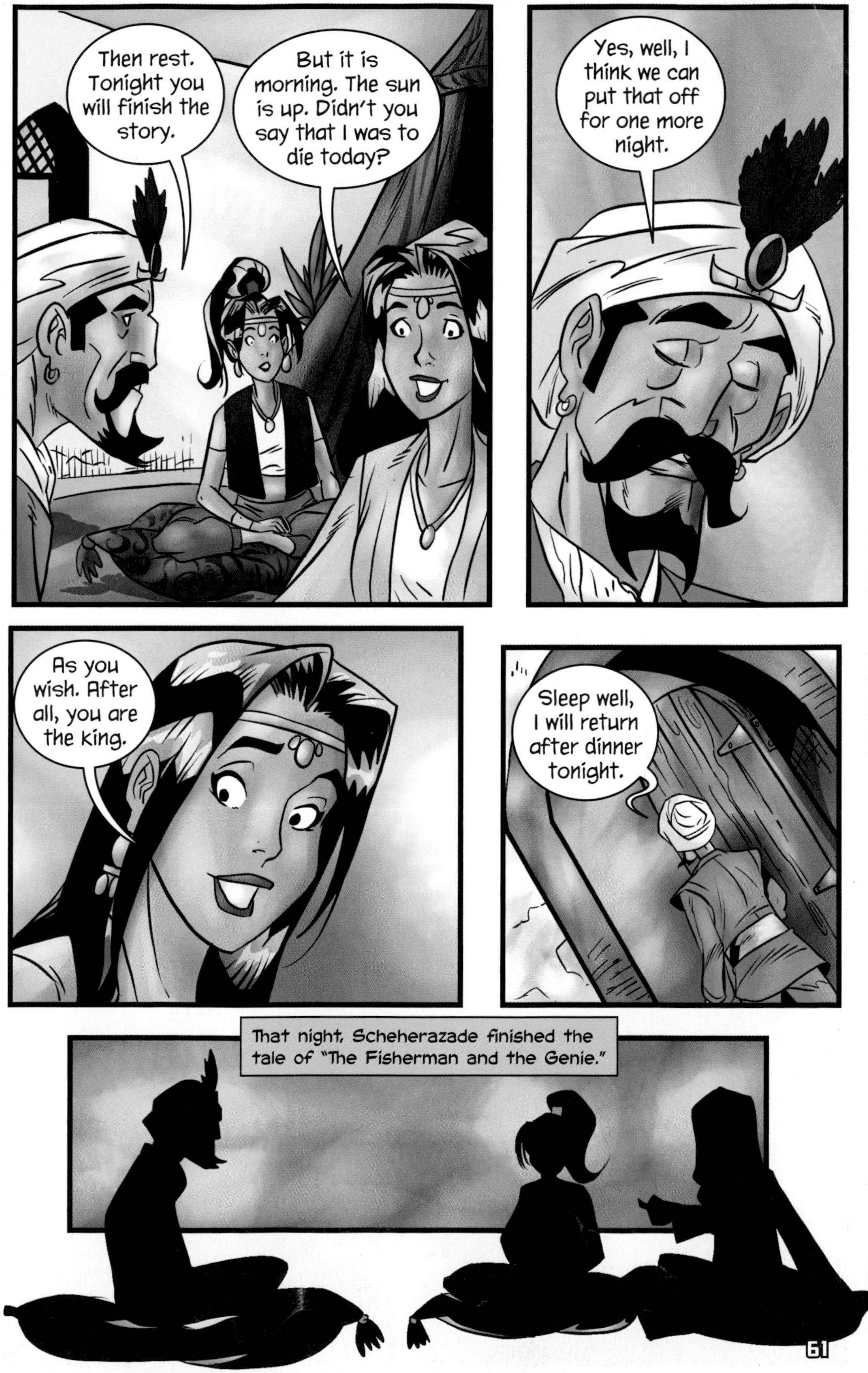
Then rest. Tonight you will finish the story.
But it is morning. The sun is up. Didn't you say that I was to die today?
Yes, well, I think we can put that off for one more night.
As you wish. After all, you are the king.
Sleep well, I will return after dinner tonight.
That night, Scheherazade finished the tale of "The Fisherman and the Genie."

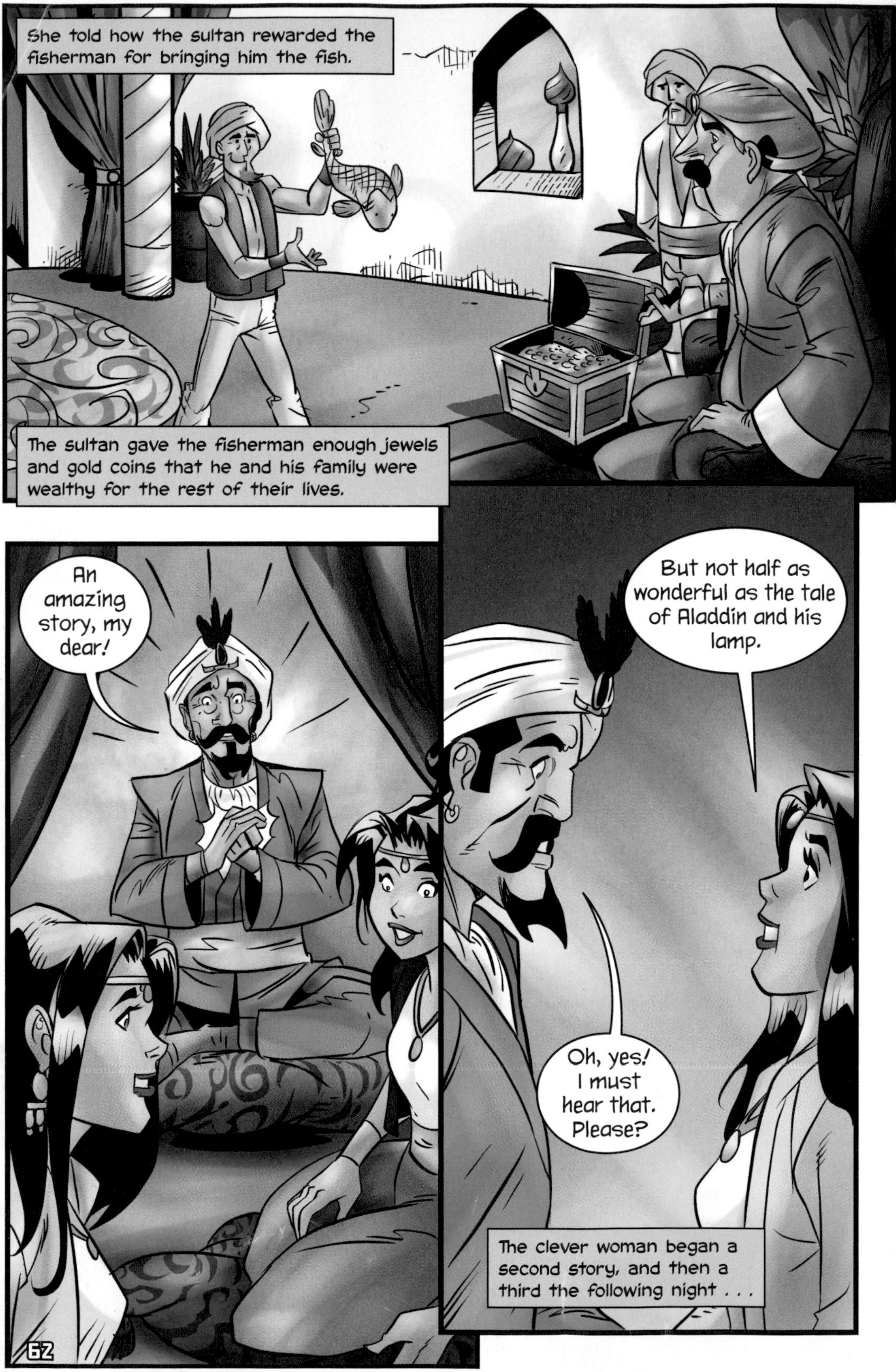
She told how the sultan rewarded the fisherman for bringing him the fish.
The sultan gave the fisherman enough jewels and gold coins that he and his family were wealthy for the rest of their lives.
An amazing story, my dear!
But not half as wonderful as the tale of Aladdin and his lamp.
Oh, yes! I must hear that. Please?
The clever woman began a second story, and then a third the following night . . .

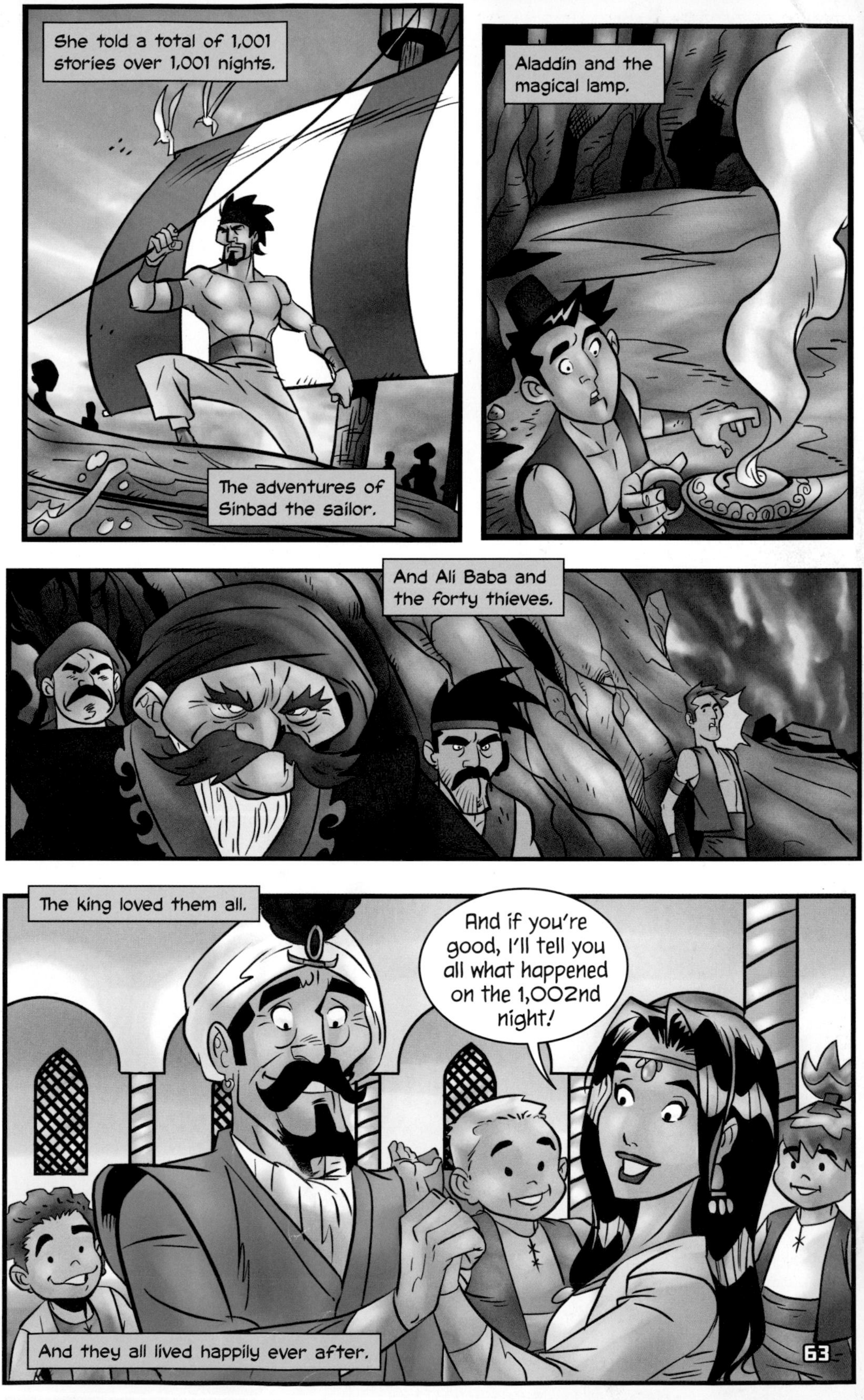
She told a total of 1,001 stories over 1,001 nights.
The adventures of Sinbad the sailor.
Aladdin and the magical lamp.
And Ali Baba and the forty thieves.
The king loved them all.
And if you're good, I'll tell you all what happened on the 1,002nd night!
And they all lived happily ever after.

ARABIAN NIGHTS

The story of "The Fisherman and the Genie" is part of a collection of Middle Eastern and South Asian folktales known as *One Thousand and One Nights*. These tales have been passed down from generation to generation for hundreds of years. The first English-language edition, titled *The Arabian Nights' Entertainment*, was published in 1706.

Since then, many versions of the book have been published — some containing more than 1,000 stories. In each of these editions, the tales of mystery and adventure are told by the same narrator, a beautiful woman named Scheherazade. She has just married an evil ruler who plans to kill her before the night is through. To stop him, Scheherazade entertains the king with a new story each night, and he soon forgets about his deadly plan.

The Arabian Nights tales remain some of the greatest stories ever told. They include popular adventures, such as "The Fisherman and the Genie," "The Seven Voyages of Sinbad," and "Ali Baba and the Forty Thieves." Many of these stories have been adapted into movies, books, and plays that are still popular today.

MORE ABOUT GENIES

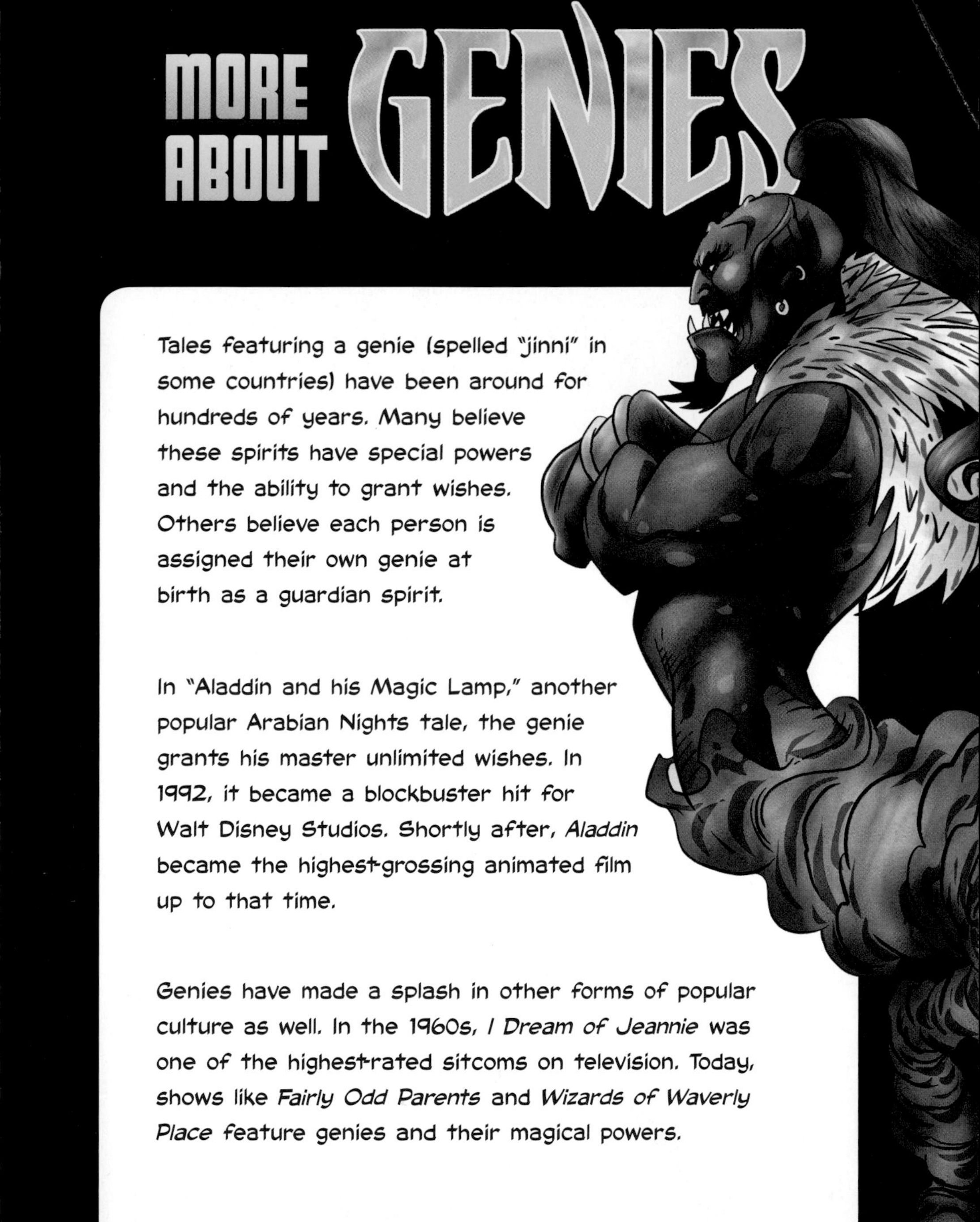

Tales featuring a genie (spelled "jinni" in some countries) have been around for hundreds of years. Many believe these spirits have special powers and the ability to grant wishes. Others believe each person is assigned their own genie at birth as a guardian spirit.

In "Aladdin and his Magic Lamp," another popular Arabian Nights tale, the genie grants his master unlimited wishes. In 1992, it became a blockbuster hit for Walt Disney Studios. Shortly after, *Aladdin* became the highest-grossing animated film up to that time.

Genies have made a splash in other forms of popular culture as well. In the 1960s, *I Dream of Jeannie* was one of the highest-rated sitcoms on television. Today, shows like *Fairly Odd Parents* and *Wizards of Waverly Place* feature genies and their magical powers.

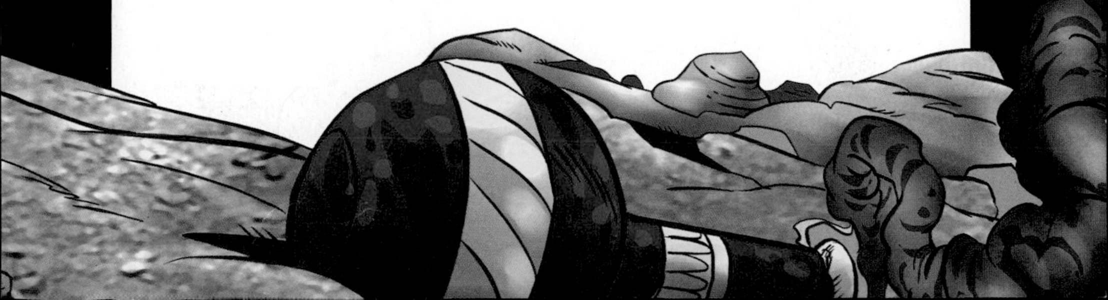

ABOUT THE AUTHOR

Eric Fein is a freelance writer and editor. He has written
dozens of comic book stories featuring The Punisher,
Spider-Man, Iron Man, Conan, and even Godzilla. He has
also written more than forty books and graphic novels for
educational publishers. As an editor, Eric has worked on
books featuring Spider-Man, Venom, and Batman, as well as
several storybooks, coloring and activity books, and how-to-
draw books.

ABOUT THE ILLUSTRATOR

Eduardo Garcia has illustrated for magazines around the
world, including ones in Italy, France, United States, and
Mexico. Eduardo loves working for publishers like Marvel
Comics, Stone Arch Books, and Idea + Design Works,
and BOOM! Studios. Eduardo has illustrated many great
characters like Speed Racer, the Spider-Man family, Kade,
and others. Eduardo is married to his beloved wife, Nancy M.
Parrazales. They have one son, the amazing Sebastian Inaki,
and an astonishing dog named Tomas.

GLOSSARY

advisor (ad-VIZE-or)—someone who gives information or suggestions to a king or other leader

cast (KAST)—to throw a fishing line or net into the water

forbid (fur-BID)—to order someone not to do something

genie (JEE-nee)—in tales from the Middle East, a genie is a spirit who obeys the person who summons it and grants the person's wishes

grateful (GRAYT-fuhl)—thankful for something that you are given

imprisonment (im-PRIZ-uhn-ment)—being locked in prison

mast (MAST)—a tall pole that stands on the deck of a ship or boat and supports its sail

quarters (KWOR-turz)—lodging, or rooms where people live

request (ri-KWEST)—something that you ask for politely

sultan (SUHLT-uhn)—an emperor or ruler of some Muslim countries

valuable (VAL-yuh-buhl)—worth a lot of money

vow (VOU)—to make a serious or important promise

DISCUSSION QUESTIONS

1. Why do you think Scheharazade chose to marry the evil king? Do you think it was a good idea? Why or why not?

2. Do you think the fisherman should have opened the mysterious jar? Why or why not?

3. The genie offered the fisherman one last request. If you could have one wish, what would you ask for?

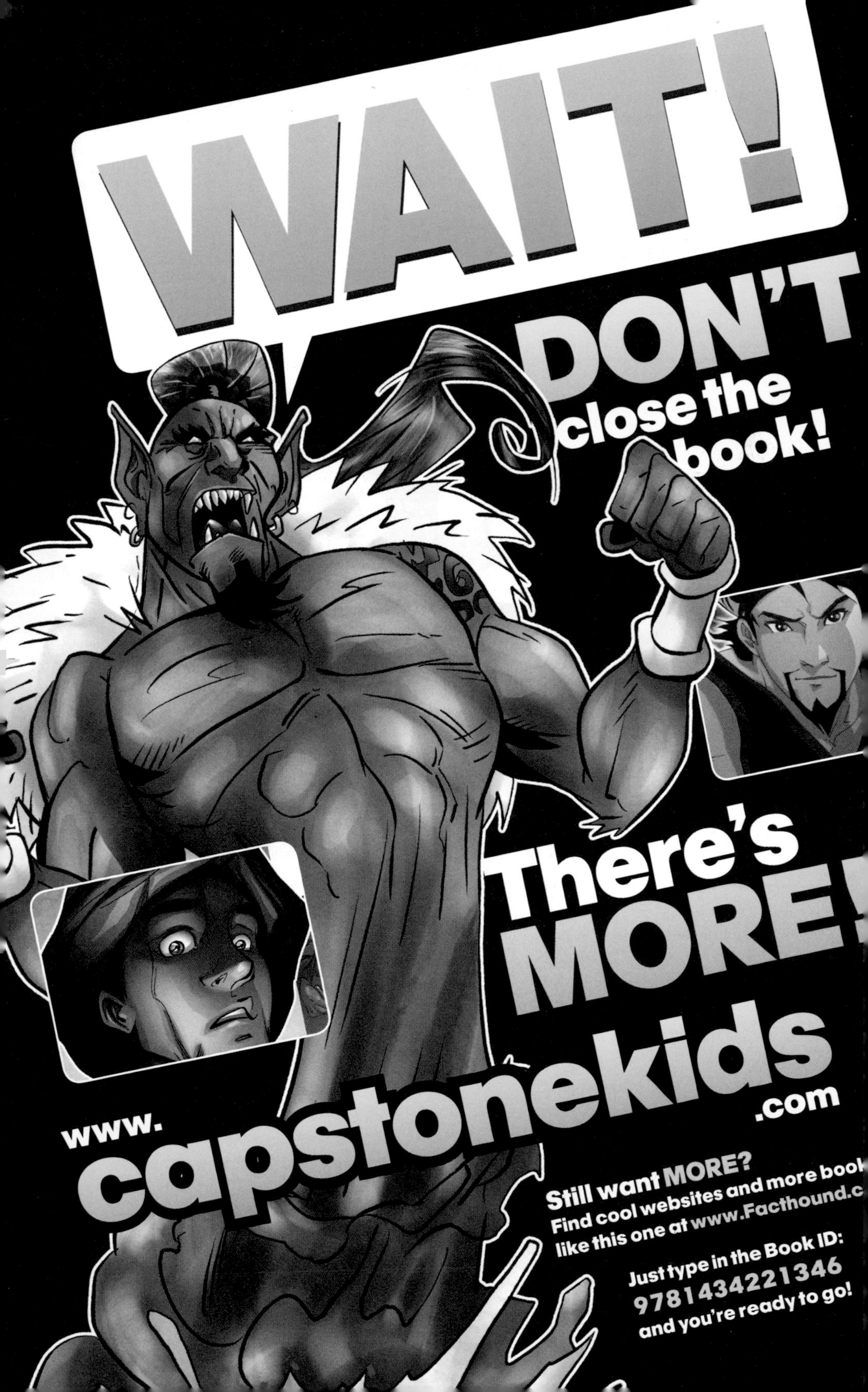
WAIT!
DON'T close the book!
There's MORE
www.capstonekids.com
Still want MORE?
Find cool websites and more book
like this one at www.Facthound.c
Just type in the Book ID:
9781434221346
and you're ready to go!

ARABIAN NIGHTS TALES!

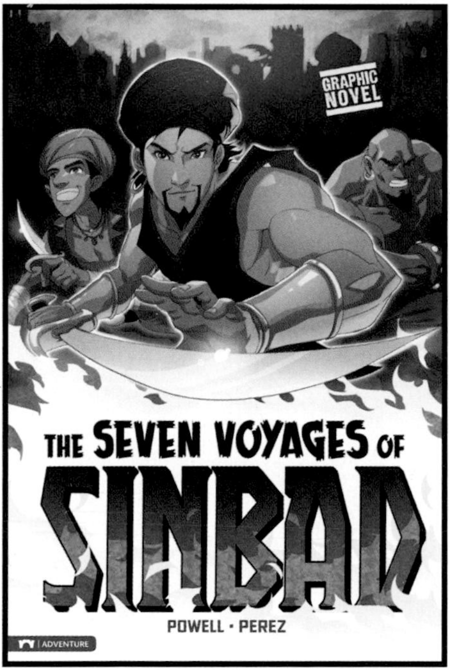
GRAPHIC NOVEL
THE SEVEN VOYAGES OF
SINBAD
POWELL · PEREZ
ADVENTURE

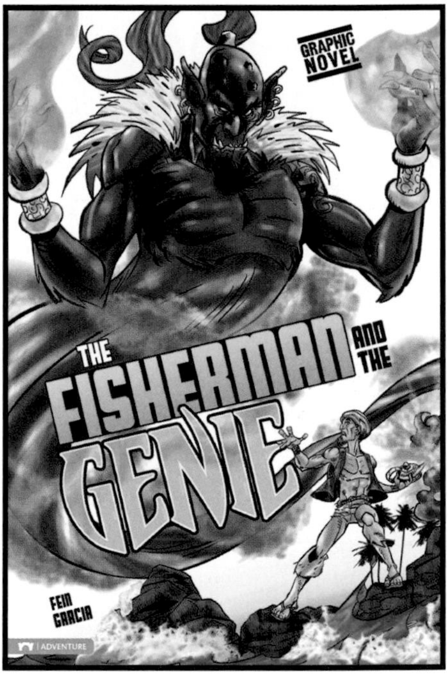
GRAPHIC NOVEL
THE
FISHERMAN AND THE
GENIE
FEIN
GARCIA
ADVENTURE

THE SEVEN VOYAGES OF SINBAD

The tale of Sinbad the Sailor, who goes to sea in search of great riches and discovers even greater adventures. On his seven treacherous voyages, the Persian explorer braves a shipwreck, fights off savage cannibals, and battles a giant Cyclops, hoping to survive and tell his legendary story.

FISHERMAN AND THE GENIE

The legendary tale of an evil Persian king, who marries a new wife each day and then kills her the next morning. To stop this murderous ruler, a brave woman named Scheherazade risks her own life and marries the king herself . . . but not without a plan. On their wedding night, she will entertain him with the tale of the Fisherman and the Genie — a story so amazing, he'll never want it to end.

WRITING PROMPTS

1. Make a list of three wishes. Then write one paragraph describing how you could make each of these wishes come true.

2. Imagine your own Arabian Nights tale. Think of a story filled with mystery and adventure. Then write it down and read it to friends and family.

3. Graphic novels are often written and illustrated by two different people. Write a story, and then give it to a friend to illustrate the pictures.

STONE ARCH BOOKS

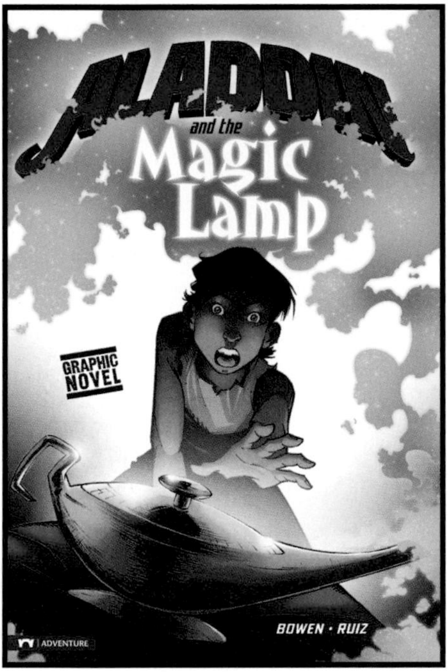
ALADDIN
and the
Magic Lamp
GRAPHIC NOVEL
BOWEN · RUIZ
ADVENTURE

ALADDIN AND THE MAGIC LAMP

The legendary tale of Aladdin, a poor youth living in the city of Al Kal'as. One day, the crafty boy outsmarts an evil sorcerer, getting his hands on a magical lamp that houses a wish-fulfilling genie! Soon, all of Aladdin's dreams come true, and he finds himself married to a beautiful princess. All is well until, one day, the evil sorcerer returns to reclaim the lamp.

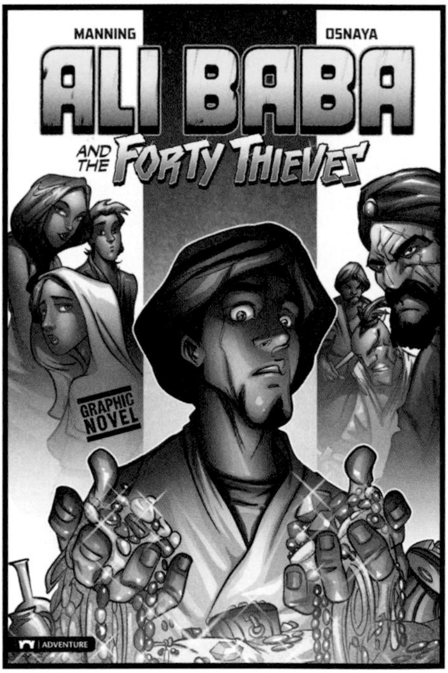
MANNING
OSNAYA
ALI BABA
AND THE FORTY THIEVES
GRAPHIC NOVEL
ADVENTURE

ALI BABA AND THE FORTY THIEVES

The legendary tale of Ali Baba, a young Persian boy who discovers a cave filled with gold and jewels, the hidden treasures of forty deadly thieves. Unfortunately, his greedy brother, Kasim, cannot wait to get his hands on the riches. Returning to the cave, he is captured by the thieves and killed, and now the evil men want revenge on Ali Baba as well.